W9-DHU-014

DISCARDED

The Odyssey of Henry Ford and the Great Peace Ship

Burnet Hershey

TAPLINGER PUBLISHING COMPANY

New York

Taplinger Publishing Co., Inc.
29 East Tenth Street
New York, New York, 10003

To MONABELLE

Published simultaneously in the Dominion of Canada by Burns & MacEachern, Ltd., Toronto

Library of Congress Catalogue Card Number 67-17122

Manufactured in the United States of America

Acknowledgments

My profound gratitude—which is only a small measure of my debt—is extended to the many who have shared with me in the arduous task of assembling, collating and editing the material for this volume. I especially want to mention May Dikeman Hoss whose judgment and contributions have been invaluable; Ruth Nathan, whose research and editorial advice was indispensable and my friend and fellow-survivor Louis Lochner, who reached into his memory as chief abettor to aid me in this exercise of total recall.

Contents

Introduction

In the winter of 1915, I was a nineteen-year-old rookie reporter covering Police Headquarters and general assignments in Manhattan for the *Brooklyn Eagle*. One day, the assistant managing editor, a tall lanky Harvard man named Hans von Kaltenborn, emitting a louder grunt than usual, asked me to fin1 out what was happening in room 717 at the Biltmore Hotel, New York. He said Henry Ford had set up "Peace Headquarters" there and was about to tell the press what his peace plans for ending the war in Europe were all about.

At this time, one must remember that America was a singularly innocent country, looking on at the muddled European scene with something like wide-eyed astonishment and naïveté, or as some disapproving theatre-goer who watches a vulgar melodrama. The death struggle along the Western front was in its early stages; the Marne had played its glorious prologue, and the stage was being set at Verdun for an unforgettable drama. The American public read the European headlines with mild interest before going on to the sports news where the box score, at least, was reliable.

Henry Ford was not so detached. When I met him I found he was burning with a plan that would "put a stop to the silly killings going on abroad." He felt the warring nations had fought long enough, and that America, as an onlooking power, should step in and ask them to kiss and make up. Since the country was still professing neutrality and revelling in its "splendid isolation," Ford had no hope that the United States

government would consider itself in the role of a peace media-
tor. No, he declared passionately, it was plainly up to him. "If
I can make automobiles run, why can't I steer those people clear
of war?" he cried with the most guileless super-confidence.

Unlike my colleagues, most of whom were older and more
cynical, I was inclined to take the peace expedition seriously
and, consequently, when I got to my typewriter, after the
visit to the Biltmore, I treated the story with considerable rev-
erence. Very earnestly, I quoted Mr. Ford's happy thought
(contributed by a press agent) of "getting the boys out of the
trenches by Christmas." An inspiring idea, I said to myself.

The hard-boiled Park Row fraternity took an entirely different slant. To them, this was another Ford-inspired joke, like
the tin lizzie gags which had invaded the world.

My editor, equally hardboiled, nevertheless allowed me to
take a grave view of the whole affair, and, with all the editorial bias possible in a news column, I took my stand in favor
of Peace and Henry Ford. These were the first pangs of a
youthful and idealistic *weltschmertz* that was destined to get
me into a lot of trouble for the next half century.

My pro-peace enthusiasms evidently attracted the attention
of the Peace Ship organizers, so Ford sent me a telegram, a
week before the sailing from Hoboken, New Jersey, and invited me to join the newspaper delegation on the Peace Ship,
Oscar II.

If only for its value as a piece of incredible Americana, this
is a glance backward at the almost wistfully pathetic attempt
to bring peace to an anguished world at war. Not that very
many saw anything wistful or pathetic in it then, on that December 4th 1915.

B.H.

New York, *1967*

1

Oh, What an Unlovely War

But we can't let this happen! Over America, the cry went up. This was not the theoretical protest of pacifists. This was a reflexive outcry, as the shots that shook Europe ricocheted through the heart of America.

To Americans in 1915 Europe was everything, had everything. The smallest continent was the moral home of the world. For most Americans some part of Europe was called home, because there were

> The ashes of his fathers
> and the temples of his Gods.

Europe was the security behind America's lighthearted ways. *There* was art, there was philosophy, the Church, science, invention, money. And this stronghold of all the western world's great traditions was also the source of the powerful movements of reform. What more was there to civilization?

We see now what nobody saw then. The fount from which all things flowed was full of fissures. The lines had long since been drawn. It was Germany and Austria-Hungary and Italy on the one hand, and Russia and France, Britain and Japan on the other. The trap of alliances—that spurious "Balance of Power"—was set.

History is bunk! as one typical—and not so typical—American declared. This observation was characteristic at least of its laconic pacifist author, Henry Ford. But no less a thinker than the noted jurist, the late Judge Jerome Frank, has since added, "It would be better for us today if we had heeded Henry Ford."

In all history there had never been such a "Balance of Power" before. Neither had there truly been a *World* War.

Many knowledgeable men in those days were saying that the Nineteenth century really ended in 1914. What they meant was that the flavor of life which existed before Sarajevo was still permeating the early years of the new century, and what was good of the *fin de siécle* continued to be savored along with the improved and wider uses of electricity, telephones and automobiles.

In France this writer found that the people had barely shaken off the cataclysmic effects of the Dreyfus case. In fact, I had seen and was introduced to the medal-bedecked Colonel Dreyfus in Paris, as he entered the Rothschild Temple on the Rue de la Victoire for the Jewish High Holy Day services of Yom Kippur.

The commotion of the Affair had died down, but most of the senior army men, the judges and journalists were still present. Anatole France and Georges Clemenceau were at the height of their vigor. Marcel Proust was to be seen dining in solitary elegance at the Cafe d'Angleterre; Debussy and Degas were flesh and blood Parisians in daily evidence. Claude Monet at 75, white beard and inverness cape, and his 76-year-old partner in the great Impressionist plot, Pierre Auguste Renoir, were around preparing for their immortality.

The return to the main boulevards of the horse-drawn buses (there was a shortage of petrol), the still active Moulin Rouge and Bal Tabarin, the unchanged Latin Quarter and the still standing remnants of the Paris Exposition—all were testimony of a century that had just passed, but which was resisting rigor mortis. Nevertheless, the *ancien* regime was in its terminal stage, expiring in the rubble made by the German guns. Paris, home of the first neon lights, had blacked out.

The shadow of the eclipse spread over the world.

America still pranced in the afterglow of her own Gay Nineties. Paris was dark, but Broadway dazzled with the Ziegfeld Follies of 1915, with Victor Herbert's tulle-and-tinsel *Princess Pat*, with Jerome Kern, with the Horatio Parker prize opera *Fairyland* and Jean Webster's *Daddy Longlegs*. For the "longhairs" of 1915, there was Isadora Duncan letting down all of hers, and, worse than that!—baring her feet, in *Oedipus Rex;* there was gutsy drama—*Blood Is Thicker than Water* and *Common Clay*. For those who thrilled to melodrama in a high key, there was *Madame Butterfly;* there was Caruso.

But even as the show went on for Americans, shadows of the darkness in Europe crept across the stage.

The new Hal Caine drama, *The Manxman*, landed in trouble when the actors didn't want to sail over submarine-infested waters. With the forecast that Italians would be called up for active service, members of the Metropolitan Opera staff fell away. Toscanini refused to come back to the United States and had to be replaced. In the world of high fashion, dominated by the military modes sweeping Paris, controversy raged over the question of unlined clothing for men and high heels for women, and in the Easter Parade of 1915, the cynosure of eyes was the feet rather than the head—for spats rivalled hats.

So much for America's great cosmopolitan centers which were reflectors, if in spots and blots, of the flares and shades of the holocaust in Europe. Over rural America, beginning to be linked by Henry Ford's direct-communication Model T, the shadow spread more slowly, insidiously.

As for the world of art, it was the United States which gave refuge to the rebellious French ideas, such as Dadaism. Marcel

Duchamp, who had scored a *success de scandale* with his "Nude Descending on Staircase" at the Armory Show two years earlier (1913), had burst on the '15 scene with his signal work of the day, "painted" in strips of copper between deliberately-cracked glass. It was titled "Bride Stripped Bare by her Bachelors Even." (The "Bachelors" were the gendarme, the cuirassier, the city policeman, the priest, the bellhop, the delivery boy, the flunky, the undertaker's man, and the station master.) Typical of famous canvases of this genre in 1915 was Giorgio de Chirico's "The Seer," an armless, eggheaded figure with cyclops eye, in breastplate and danseur's tights, turns aside from a blackboard chalked with perspectives.

Reality was too much. But in their very flight into Dadaism, Cubism and those other fist-shakings at a classical, even impressionist old fogyism, the artists mirrored a fractionalized world. In the dismembered parts of the art of 1915 we see the very world the artists fled, crying "This is too much!" Yet in their very "escape," they gave us fragments of machines, of human beings, and of human life itself.

But the average man was not an artist. He was that eternal pragmatic soul who sought to *cope,* to come to grips with the imponderable, the war. And these practical people did their part, with a will and with a vengeance.

There sprang up enough "societies" to fill a special wartime classified directory. It was every man for himself, according to his own temperament and predilections, with his own answer to a single cry:

"What can we *do?*"

The cry had gone up all over America, as people watched the world fall apart—not just the real world, but their ideal world, the world that *was,* and that in a sense never was.

They witnessed atrocity—the "rape of Belgium," the technique of *spurlos versenkt,* sinking without trace. Both credulously and in disbelief, America looked at the retouched war posters showing the Belgian child with his arms apparently hacked off, and asked, where was the homeland of *Faust,* of Fichte, of Heine, the *gemutliche* beer-garden, the gay students, the strains of "Wiener Blut" and "Artist's Life?" The intellectual, professorial sector were asking more searching, but none the less perturbing questions about "law and international morality," the "rights of neutrals," and the inviolability of treaties—now called "scraps of paper"—and were loudly ventilating their bitterness and indignation. If, in 1915, the Belgian front no longer was the principal setting for the clash of arms, the Belgian "cause" stayed on as the polemic controversy of the day to become the principal asset of Allied propaganda.

With their characteristic failure to read historical portent, the Germans had underestimated the determination of the Belgians to resist aggression. Characteristically, they had also neglected to foresee the violent revulsion which the invasion of a small peaceful country (whose integrity they had themselves guaranteed) would provoke in other countries. Not only England was aroused. It affected neutrals, too, who, sooner or later, were to enter the struggle, such as Italy, Rumania and the United States. It evoked hostile feelings in countries like Holland and Scandinavia, on which Germany depended for her food supply. The violation of Belgian neutrality, on the pretext of "military necessity," became a test case. It was felt almost everywhere that a German victory would spell the end of independence of all European states which did not submit to German domination.

For Americans the question was thus narrowed to Germany's responsibility for betraying a solemn treaty, and taking an unfair advantage of the trust placed in her signature. Both sides, Americans agreed, pursued rival policies and stock-piled armaments, but Germany alone had violated its pledge. It had also violated the ordinary, accepted rules of warfare.

Liege and Louvain were headline names in 1915, and they had the same effect on average minds as did Lidice and Coventry a quarter of a century later. Liege evoked the noble figure of old General Leman; Louvain, the destruction of a unique library and of one of Europe's most ancient seats of learning. The lawless character of the assault was compounded by its unexpected cruelty.

Popular imagination was easily moved by simple facts. As an American put it at the time, "The Belgian story was as good as a play." This is perhaps why some people ceased to believe in it. In the light of after-war cynicism, it seemed almost too good to be true to those who had not witnessed it. The power-mad Kaiser appeared on the world screens at the side of the tall heroic blonde King of the Belgians, against a background of smoking ruins. Heroes cropped up all over the country. Silent film versions of their heroism were being shown around the world. There was Burgomaster Max, who refused to yield to the enemy's exactions and stirred the spirit of Brussels, and Cardinal Mercier's great Pastoral Letter of Christmas 1914, preaching "Patriotism and Fortitude." There was Nurse Edith Cavell—the British "Florence Nightingale," who was publicly executed by the ruthless Prussians—forerunners of the S.S. and Nazi war criminals. She became one of the first significant martyrs of World War I when she uttered her last words before the German firing squad: "Patriotism is not enough."

Stop it! was America's cry to Europe and to herself. It was the involuntary command of a people who felt that they *could* stop a holocaust. This was the faith America possessed in 1915.

Perhaps the rallying cry of the jingoists and the call of the pacifists were but two sides of the same coin. In the old jingle, "We've got the men, we've got the guns, we've got the money, too," the essence was that messianic feeling, "It's up to us!" The faith that America could save the world, whether with guns or mediation, was based on the root, if of all evil, of most faith, too—money. In the jingoist verse, the key word was *money*.

We've got the money, too. What American especially had it? None other than the pacifist industrial emperor, Henry Ford.

When he asked, "What can we do?" people *told* him. Better than that, or worse, he told *himself*. The messianic spirit of America's Age of Innocence was polarized in Henry Ford. He could afford to carry it off.

"You can't do a durned thing," might have been a typical Ford pronouncement after it was all over, although he never admitted it. But no one ever has admitted that war cannot be stopped, and that the answer is "Not a thing" to the cry, then or now, of "What can we *do?*"

"Nice try, Henry," was the gist of the kindest things people had to say about what Ford did. This was rather an understatement.

"War to End Christmas Day; Ford to Stop It," read a news headline in December, 1915.

The nationwide cry of *Stop it!* had been taken up by Ford. He would stop the war, if he had to go to do it in person, taking with him as much of America as he could get, and if he had to hire an ocean ship. Ford's answer to "What can we do?" was exactly that.

In those times of transition just before the takeover by mass media, while America still had its private life, for better or worse, Coxey's Army rode again. The Henry Ford Peace Expedition was a last splurge of Americana, pure and simple, powered by a fortune, a faith, and a cry which has never been answered yet. *Stop the war!*

2

The Ship of Foolish Peace Pilgrims

Dirty weather overhung the Hoboken pier. But the early December freezing drizzle, beyond which the jagged Manhattan skyline of the year 1915 loomed as a mirage, failed to dampen the uproar. The pilings lurched and creaked against the weight of a crowd of 1,500.

The Captain of the Danish Peace Ship named Oscar II of the Scandinavian-American Line that Henry Ford had chartered, announced that the vessel would get underway at 2 p.m. that fourth day of December, 1915. But since before noon the dock had been mobbed. And it was an occasion when "All ashore who's going ashore," was an ambiguous command. The minds of some were made up for them by burly Danish crewmen acting as bouncers.

On deck, Henry Ford, dapper in sable-collared overcoat, derby hat and walking stick, made a last plea to his beloved crony, Thomas Edison.

"Tom, will you take a million dollars to come along?"

"It sure is, Henry," replied the aging Edison, who, even without the uproar, was very deaf.

8

Henry Ford with his crony, Tom Edison. WIDE WORLD PHOTOS.

"I say, will you come with me for a million dollars!" shouted Ford, above the roar of the boat whistles and clanging gear and chain.

Edison smiled affectionately. He was one of many who never got Ford's message, for all the money.

But there were plenty of takers.

Applicants for the voyage included the president of the Anti-Smoking League, the author of "I didn't Raise My Boy to Be a Soldier," and a woman who had torn 10,000 bandages for the Belgians.

Represented on the pier was every extremist group in America: the pacifists, the jingoists, the "Dry" party, the I.W.W. (Industrial Workers of the World, also called the Wobblies) and every religious splinter-group. A German contingent arrived from the *Bier Stube* back of the Hoboken waterfront, and their singing of "Deutschland, Deutschland, Uber Alles" was counterpointed vigorously by the "Marseillaise" and "God Save the King" from French and British partisans. The peace advocates unfurled a banner showing St. George and the dragon— the champion of peace crushing war. They sang

> There would be no more war
> If every mother'd say,
> "I didn't raise my boy to be a soldier" . . .

and the band aboard ship responded with a rendition of the Danish national anthem. Few recognized it. Women shrieked and fainted. An epileptic suffered a *grand mal* seizure. Peace delegates and their well-wishers or ill-wishers came at closest range in a struggle to identify luggage, which the crowd, as well as reporters and photographers jockeying for position, were standing on.

But the turmoil and the dirty weather in Hoboken were only dim reflections of the storm raging over Europe, into which the Henry Ford Peace Expedition was perilously sailing, and which it hoped to quell.

All was not so quiet on the Western front, despite what the celebrated military "critics" Liddell Hart and Frank Simmonds called a "standstill." It is true both sides had dug in—entrenched in that elaborate network of ditches stretching 600 miles across Belgium and France. But heavy artillery action was intense along the entire line.

In the newspapers the very morning of the sailing, alongside of the front-page story of the "Peace Ship," were Allied and Central Power communiques reporting a German reinforcement of the Flanders and Artois battle-lines, in readiness for a blow at those sectors; a French admission that the Germans had seized 800 feet of trenches near Auberive and the Russians had suffered a blow to their entrenchments at Dvina. The British were bogged down in the snow and mud of northern France, stunned by that first German poison gas attack at Ypres and still reeling from the disaster to their morale by the "Dunkirk" at Gallipoli. It was the year of the trench, and medical jargon acquired two new *noms de guerre* for two of its oldest diseases: trench mouth and trench feet. Together with poison gas and "Spanish flu," these four accounted for more casualties than shrapnel.

While it was more touch than go on land, as the Oscar II weighed anchor for its peace offensive, the seas were ablaze with naval disasters. Allied cruisers were hit three times that week; the British steamships Middleton and Clan Macleod were sunk in the Mediterranean, and the Swedish S.S. Norvick was sunk by a mine.

A momentary epidemic of cold feet spread through the ranks of the more timid of the passenger list. It was one thing to fight for peace with resolutions and speeches and pamphlets, but who wants a wintry grave in the North Atlantic? There were a few last-minute cancellations from among the delegates, but the rank and file stuck, as did the intrepid newspaper reporters and, of course, the contingent of youth from the colleges, who were in full rehearsal for the "flaming" era acoming. Only their parents were worried about the U-boats. Some were tearful as they said their good-byes on the pier. It was not difficult sympathizing with the panic of these students' parents, when right there on the pier newsboys' voices loudly hawked: "Extra, extra!—Germans sink ocean liner! . . . hundreds drown!"

On the diplomatic front that week, belligerent activity

matched the actual battle scene. The London press declared that the German army and navy must be destroyed. George Bernard Shaw, master of the quotable quote, was being quoted to the effect that "the Allies' own *Drang nach Osten* was to fight to Berlin!" The Quadruple Entente war board met at Calais, after pledging "no separate peace," and appealed for "comfort kits" for the fighting men. Comfort in Europe had reached a new low.

Various campaigns to whip up American feeling were reported in the newspapers that morning. Mrs. Whitney Warren, socialite wife of the noted architect, held speaking engagements on her tour of devastated France. The Paderewski doll auction at Manhattan's Hotel Gotham was dedicated to Polish war relief. The glamorous jet-haired, blue-eyed prima donna, Irish-American Geraldine Farrar sang concerts for German benefit. It was the era of the "hyphenated American."

Publisher R. H. Rand of the *London Daily Mail* calculated that the war was costing England a million dollars an hour. An abstract controversy raged over R. T. Morris' theory of enzymes as the cause of war. Espionage suspicion was rampant. As the Peace Ship sailed, charges were brought against a Mrs. Caroline G. Bartlett, alleged spy for Germany, where she was called "Sister Beatrice."

Meanwhile, astronomical observatories charted a new comet. It seems fitting that the celestial patron of the Ford Expedition should be a shooting star, flamboyant and fleeting. But unlike the ballyhooed Peace Ship, its heavenly counterpart rose and fell unnoted by the public, a casualty of censorship.

The actual onslaught of the Henry Ford Peace Expedition against this chaos of conflict was almost spontaneous. The pacifist movement had fully come into its own. Ford's own anti-militant stance was well established. But practical events and personal confrontations directly culminating in the scene at the Hoboken pier moved in pace with the ideal of an automobile manufacturer—speed.

On the one hand, this was to take the headlocked world by surprise. On the other hand, the Expedition took its own delegates and even its patron by surprise as well.

As far as his sentiments on war went, Henry Ford had laid it on the line in numerous interviews:

"Take away the capitalists and you will sweep war from the earth."

"It is only through misapprehension that men will fight each other."

"For those who remain at the end of the sad folly, there are high taxes and death at the door."

This was the terse talk of a master showman—or entrepreneur, for Ford was suddenly diffident when placed center stage. The impact of homely aphorisms like these hit hard, far and wide. Conflict makes strange bedfellows. Many crossing paths bent to converge upon the Detroit motor king. Ford's native Dearborn was the mecca of all sorts and conditions of pacifists.

Finally Ford got down to figures. "I would spend half my fortune to shorten the war by one day."

This more personal Ford epigram was soon to be seized upon by the first of all the newsmen to exploit Ford's pacifism. Theodore Delavigne, an obscure leg-man for the *Detroit Free Press,* cornered the Ford story. He catapulted himself to the front page, and he made idol Henry Ford (or victim, as some saw it) the man to see.

Delavigne got "in" with Ford in the first place through one of those fortuities which were to form the fabric of the whole adventure. The young newsman happened to have been previously acquainted in Baltimore with a skilled jeweler, from whom he had picked up a good deal of incidental knowledge in the craft. In Ford's presence, Delavigne identified by its workmanship an Italian mantle clock at a distance of thirty feet. With Henry Ford, this was all it took. Delavigne must have the kind of sharpness Ford respected. In the *Detroit Free Press,* he accordingly became Ford's mouthpiece, and coined the paper's most effective headlines.

"Millions Are Murdered by Military Parasites"—"Cannon and Slaughter No Part of Patriotism"—"Sloths and Lunatics in Military Clique"—"Public Must Control Action of Rulers" —"People of All Lands Cry Out Against War"—"Henry Ford to Push World-Wide Campaign for Universal Peace—Devote Life and Fortune to Combat Spirit of Militarism Now Rampant."

And how was this grandiose plan to be implemented?

In the first place, the plan was to be based on the Neutral Conference for Continuous Mediation document, originated by the prodigious Mme. Rosika Schwimmer of Hungary, and embodied in the resolution of the Chicago Emergency Peace Conference of February 1915.

This set forth the classic idea, as old as war itself, that one must perpetuate a situation in which no one has thrown in the sponge and there is no loss of prestige or face. Translation: Mediation. Another of its prime points was that a peace must not humiliate, and must not tend to renewal of hostilities.

Heading the "Continuous Mediation" disciples in the United States was the gifted young writer, Louis P. Lochner; Jane Addams, founder of Hull House; and Dr. David Starr Jordan, President Emeritus of Stanford University, ichthyologist, and head of the American Peace Society. It was in Jordan's company that Lochner first met President Woodrow Wilson for personal presentation of the Continuous Mediation plan. Wilson, the idealist—but ever the astute politician—blew hot with sympathy and cold with commitment.

"Maybe it was me," lamented Jordan, the incurable punster academician whose fame as an ichthyologist was wide. "Maybe he feels there is something fishy going on."

Thereupon burst upon the scene of disappointment and frustration, like a catalyst, the mother of the plan, Mme. Rosika Schwimmer. To Mme. Schwimmer's capabilities discreet Emily

Mme. Rosika Schwimmer, who originated the scheme. GREELEY
PHOTO SERVICE.

Balch paid somewhat ambiguous tribute. Miss Balch who
characterized herself as an "improper" Bostonian, a leading
feminist and social worker, apostrophized Mme. Schwimmer as
one "to whom nothing human is alien"—which is certainly to
cover a great deal. Then she proceeded to add, no doubt without wishing to attribute to her sister-pacifist a touch of the
gypsy, that "Mme. Schwimmer is politically a *Hungarian*."

Mme. Schwimmer, indeed the Hungarian delegate to the International Conference of Women at The Hague of April, 1915,
brought with her from the eclectically Moorish atmosphere of
the Dierentuin Hall, something of the cloak-and-dagger tradition of international politics. But this wasn't the only aspect of
Mme. Schwimmer. She was also recalled as a cosy, hausfrau

type, homey as a crock of pfeffernusse. Certainly she was selfless in her quest. To come to America in the first place, she had pawned all her jewelry.

Her descent upon Louis P. Lochner was in the form of a mystifying telegram: "Why are you not coming to Detroit to keep the appointment made for you with Mr. Ford?" . . . Both Lochner's and Mme. Schwimmer's ultimate meetings with Ford were fraught with intricacies which seemed to strike a prophetic keynote.

In the first place, Lochner had not been aware of the existence of an appointment with Ford. But he assumed that an earlier telegram from Ford's headquarters had missed him and entrained for Detroit without delay. There he learned that no interview had been scheduled. But, by luck, Ford's first secretary was away, and the second secretary, more sympathetically disposed, offered to try to squeeze Lochner in after a certain Mme. Schwimmer. "This man is a victim of circumstance," the second secretary began, in introducing Lochner to Ford.

The word "victim" was all it took. Victimization evidently was a concept big in the Ford mystique; and who now was about to "victimize" whom depended upon the point of view. At any rate, Ford spontaneously invited the "victim" home.

Even more involved was the path which brought Mme. Schwimmer herself to Ford. By one story Rosika first gained entree to Ford's wife Clara, appealing to her as a mother, and Mrs. Ford prevailed upon her husband to see the "peace ambassador"; but later Clara reversed her stand, and attempted to dissuade Ford from the enterprise.

According to one version, Mme. Schwimmer, almost in despair at the impenetrable barricade of Ford secretaries, received a phone call. It was a *Detroit Journal* reporter named Yonkers, who tipped her off that she might intercept the tycoon at the factory the following day during the lunch break.

At all events, it remains unanimous that the absence, as in Lochner's case, of Ford's No. 1 secretary, an eager beaver named E. G. Liebold, provided the weak spot in the blockade. Another crucial absentee for those seeking access to Ford was his wife's spiritual advisor, the highly controversial Dr. S. S. Marquis, Dean of the Episcopal Cathedral of Detroit.

So Lochner, the brilliant young agent of the Carnegie Peace Endowment, and the vivid brunette Mme. Schwimmer paid a joint visit to the Ford home, where their host received them in the boots of a ranger, and launched into a desultory tirade against drink and tobacco. Soon leaving "the girls" together, Ford got down to cases with his young "victim," as he continued to call Lochner. "What do you think of the Hungarian idea? How much will it cost?"

It was an astoundingly productive afternoon. Ford proposed going to New York and then to Washington to see President Wilson the following day. To other "peace" callers that same day he announced his commitment to the work of the International Committee of Women.

Rosika, for her part, had worked on Mrs. Ford to good effect. The retiring and somewhat frugal Clara found herself, evidently to her own bemusement, having pledged to head a telegraph campaign by American mothers and to foot the bill to the tune of $10,000.

This good day's work was accomplished on November 19 —barely fifteen days prior to the Peace Ship's departure. Mme. Schwimmer preceded Ford and Lochner to New York that night. On the trip East the next day Ford dictated some of his sharper diatribes against "preparedness" to Lochner for delivery at a press conference. The idea of the New York stopover was that it was a natural center of publicity.

A luncheon at the McAlpin Hotel on November 21 was attended by Jane Addams, Columbia Dean George Kirchwey, Oswald Garrison Villard of *N.Y. Post* and the *Nation* and a leading liberal, and Paul Kellogg of the *Survey,* as well as some lesser lights among the pacifists. Here the actual idea of the "ship" was hinted at, half-facetiously, by Lochner. Ford snatched it up. Its very flamboyance, to which Jane Addams objected, was its attraction for the automobile king. The concept embodied tangibility, action and drama. This was for Ford. The automobile manufacturer from the Middle West —who never had crossed the ocean—would combine his maiden voyage with a great nautical moral exploration; his ship would cut a mighty swathe through the roiling waters of the world.

Using the pseudonym "Mr. Henry," Ford commenced negotiations for the charter of a ship that same afternoon. His real identity soon had to be divulged for the steamship agents to be convinced this was not an elaborate practical joke. Having had his fun with the incognito dickering, Ford left the actual closing of the deal to Mme. Schwimmer. Once any undertaking was initiated, he was ready to delegate the details and push on to the next field to conquer, in this case the White House. The S.S. Oscar II was actually chartered before Ford ever got to see the President.

Mme. Schwimmer was elated at the swift pace of the action —she said she felt as if she was in Fairyland. Nevertheless, there was a rude shock dealt that day to the old world feminist. Theodore Delavigne, now Ford's "peace secretary," had been commissioned by his patron to issue a final public statement. *"Out of the trenches by Christmas!"* was his creation. Ford seized upon it as zestfully as he had the notion of a ship. Instantly it was the slogan and watchword of the Expedition. When Mme. Schwimmer heard it, she is said to have fainted dead away.

The setting of the timeclock for the miracle at one month was the second shock she had recently sustained.

During her first meeting with Ford, he had mentioned in an aside that he knew the cause of the war—"International Jews," he said in a friendly way to his Jewish guest. "I've got the facts."

It was the all too familiar canard to the ears of a European.

Mme. Schwimmer, fresh from the land of the Esterhazys, allowed this vagary of the American millionaire to pass. Little did she suspect that some twenty years later this notion would attain its extreme form in Henry Ford's anti-semitic sheet—the *Dearborn Independent*.

At the height of the Jew-hating period in his life, I had occasion to talk with Mme. Schwimmer. She pointed out that Ford had been inoculated with the virus long before she ever met him, and that the incubation carried over into the period of the Peace Ship. Moreover, she was convinced that her relationship with him having become somewhat abrasive, to say the least, had contributed its share to the zeal with which he directed his attacks against Jews. As a trained sociologist, she was able to offer her own analysis of Ford's anti-Jewish thinking.

"I don't believe that Ford's breed of anti-semitism was either blindly emotional or cultural or religious," she reflected in a decent and detached retrospect. "I think his was a unique form of economic anti-semitism, like his hatred of Wall Street. He regards Wall Street as the ogre within the ranks of capital, as a thorn between national and foreign wealth."

Something of the same hostility was poured out toward other competitors in high places whom Ford categorized as "manipulators of wealth and power," like Jews. Thus when Louis Lochner took him to the White House to see President Wilson, the flivver king bore a chip on his shoulder. At first with the austere Wilson, Ford played "Mister Ford Goes to Washington" to the hilt. All the color of this interview was relayed to me in a tape recording by an older, more mellowed and less zealous Louis Lochner, the highly respected author of *The Goebbels Diaries* and other significant books.

During his audience with the President, Ford lolled in an armchair, with one leg dangling over the arm. He started off by telling a Ford joke, one of his personal authorship:

"I was driving by a cemetery, and I saw a huge hole being dug. I asked the grave-digger, 'Are you going to bury a whole

Louis Lochner—
the trouble-shooter.

family?' 'No,' said the grave-digger, 'This is for one man.' 'Then why so big a hole?' 'Well, you see,' said the grave-digger, 'the fellow provided in his will that he must be buried in his Ford car, because his Ford had pulled him out of every hole, and he was sure it would pull him out of the last one.' "

Wilson relaxed enough to tell one on himself, a limerick:

> For beauty I am not a star,
> There are others more handsome by far,
> But my face, I don't mind it,
> For I am behind it—
> It's the fellow in front that I jar.

After this folksy opening, Ford came to the point. If the President would appoint an official neutral commission, Ford would underwrite its expense.

The President parried with statesmanlike circumlocution and double negatives. He would not say that this was not the best plan that had yet been presented to him. Yet if a better one were to be offered tomorrow, what was he to do had he already committed himself to Ford's plan?

The language of diplomacy was unintelligible to Ford, who used straight talk himself and was normally in a position to set the tone of a discussion. He delivered himself of what Lochner was startled to hear sound like an ultimatum to the President of the United States: at 10 a.m. the next day he would give the press the story that he had chartered a ship to send peace delegates to Europe. "If you can't act," he told Wilson, "I will."

The interview closed swiftly, in some confusion. Ford's comment, to Lochner, was: "He's a small man." Far from being in awe in the presence of the President, Ford used his favorite expletive to describe the words of the chief executive—"Bunk!" he said sourly.

Ford's noisy and suddenly called press conference at the Biltmore Hotel in New York City the next morning unfortunately established a chaotic tone for his enterprise. When actually "on," before a large audience especially, Ford invariably floundered. He bewildered the mob of reporters, whose heavy attendance had overwhelmed him, with generalizations about his particular anathema, "preparedness." Ford always had an almost Franciscan affinity for birds, and he said now, "No boy would kill a bird if he didn't have a slingshot."

It remained for Lochner and liberal publisher Oswald Garrison Villard to clear up all the technical details of the basic announcement: the name of the ship, the date of sailing (only eleven days ahead), the basic purpose. Ford's most explicit statement was, "Our ship will be armed with the longest gun in the world—the Marconi" (that antediluvian reference to radio). "It will let the world know that we are bound for peace."

For the next week and a half, pure panic reigned at the Biltmore. An entire floor was reserved for the Ford party, manned by a terror-stricken emergency corps of stenographers from a Long Island Ford branch office. While telegrams and people poured to and from the Biltmore, many of Ford's guests, to whom he had given *carte blanche,* made the most of a golden opportunity to do some of their Santa Ford Christmas shopping early, and on a scale which they had never done before. A number also undertook to outfit themselves with wardrobes for the voyage commensurate with the affluence of their host.

Meanwhile, the serious business of choosing delegates and interpreting often ambiguous replies was pursued in a turmoil, with Mme. Schwimmer dominating Ford and Jane Addams in the selection. Publishers, cabinet officers and city and state officials were issued invitations, regardless of their views. Congressmen were not, because Ford wanted them to fight "preparedness" at home in Washington. The most divisive force in the nation at this time was the controversy over "preparedness," or readiness for self-defense.

The telegraphed invitations urged the recipients to be Ford's guests on a voyage terminating "at some central point, to be determined later," and announced the acceptances of Jane Addams, Thomas Edison, and John Wanamaker, none of whom actually sailed on the ship; the latter two never even accepted. Naturally, some invitations were forged by cranks, and these frauds, discovered just before sailing, had to be explained to Ford's administration. Ford's personal cronies, of course, were invited, Edison being closest to his heart.

For Mme. Schwimmer, her eagerness to secure notables, whatever her personal relations with them, vied with her private predilections. She had a long memory for both favors and slights. In this, her hour of glory both for munificence and

Cabin Passenger List.

S. S. "OSCAR II"

CAPT. J. HEMPEL

From New York, Saturday, December 4th, 1915

retribution, her ego provided a major criterion for the screening process. Thus it subsequently was claimed that she "packed the ship."

Ford wanted, for "some fellows with *sand*," a group of students. Attractive Vassar, Smith and Wellesley girls responded.

In addition to every governor, every officer in the government, every lieutenant-governor, and every college president was invited. Fortunately, in the main, most replies were negative.

Governor Hanna of North Dakota and the Lieutenant Governor of North Carolina accepted, as did pro-German ex-congressman Bartholdt of St. Louis, who signed up until told that Ford was basically pro-Ally. Judge Ben B. Lindsey of the county and juvenile courts of Denver, Colorado became a delegate. A pioneer in the application of modern psychotherapy to juvenile delinquency, he was better known as an advocate of free love than of humanitarian methods with children or of pacifism.

For the press, in day and night attendance at the Biltmore's "Stop the War Suite," there was "color" unlimited. From the stacks of telegrams and letters, it seemed that every crackpot and nut in the country wanted to get on that boat.

A millionaire junk dealer offered to help Ford buy up all the cannons and battleships of the belligerents and melt them down for scrap, which he would then resell to Ford for use in his foundries. This would surely get the boys out of the trenches! An herbalist, purporting to bear medication for all the wounds of the world, also applied at the Biltmore for passage. An application for the Papal blessing was addressed to the wrong Pope—one deceased for centuries. Roman Catholic Cardinal Gibbons' routine "God bless you" to Ford was taken as formal approval of the voyage—and so advertised.

Dr. Charles Giffin Pease, head of the Anti-Smoking League, a half century before the 1966 cancer research revelations, pursued his vocation riding street cars to snatch cigarettes from passengers' lips. He was on Mr. Ford's preferential invitation list, being a fellow oddball whom Ford admired and whom he had met through Thomas A. Edison, an avowed enemy of the "coffin nail." But when the gangplank was pulled up, Pease the anti-smoke pilgrim, was on the pier sitting on his valises, holding a rather tragi-comic press conference. Surrounded by photographers and reporters he told the sad story (now a minor classic anecdote) of how he had been obliged to cancel his trip because his mother had suddenly taken ill. The sob-sisters relished this hearts-and-flowers tid-bit, until a reporter from the *World* asked the good doctor:

"Isn't it a fact that you were put ashore after Mr. Ford found out that you were going to share a cabin with Annette Hazelton, your girl-friend?"

Good old Doctor Pease tried to explain that "Miss Hazelton" was his "secretary," and that there was nothing immoral about her accompanying him on the voyage.

It appeared that despite the confusion reigning aboard before the sailing, Ford, "shocked to the marrow" when he heard about Miss Hazelton, asked Gaston Plantiff, his New York agent, to investigate. When he learned the truth, Ford ordered "this immoral fellow" bounced off the ship. There now was plenty of smoke.

For the men writing for a pro-War and sensationalist press, not even all this was enough. All sorts of buffoonery was fabricated, but none of it topped the unbelievable horse-play that took place on that Hoboken pier. The other side of the same coin of the American age of innocent idealism, in which the Expedition was conceived, was a ruthless carnival iconoclasm. Sane voices to rebuke those who yell "*Jump!*" to a man out on a ledge were few, and they were not the voices the public was believed to want to hear.

William Jennings Bryan was said to appear less fazed than other notables on the Hoboken pier. But the silver-tongued orator had played the Chatauqua circuits alongside Swiss yodelers and female impersonators. In that hard school of a grassroots sophomoric America, wrestling in full view of all with the inner conflicts of maturation, he had learned his imperturbability. But the press, in a kind of mutual exploitation, was dedicated to the element in the American temper of the period that was out for a good time at any cost. The cost to the

Peace Expedition, and, in the assessment of some pacifists, to peace itself, could not be calculated.

Some natures rose above all the tumult. Ida Tarbell, the Lincoln biographer, presented her declined invitation to Ford personally. And, in closing a warmly appreciative letter of several pages, Helen Keller, unable to accept Ford's invitation because of her speaking schedule, wrote to him:

> If the men in the trenches lay down their arms on Christmas day, the era of freedom will have begun. Men will never again be slaves or bare their heads to men or gods or devils.

Smaller, or merely more realistic souls, however, were fatally intimidated by the brutal scourging of public ridicule. John Wanamaker, far from unsympathetic, evaluated the enterprise thus: "A mission of generous heart, fat pocketbook, but no plan." Judge Alton B. Parker, on the other hand, called Ford "a mountebank and clown." Theodore Roosevelt, himself a Nobel Peace Prize winner, was variously quoted as condemning the Expedition as "mischievous because ridiculous" or "*not* mischievous only because ridiculous."

Among prominent personages who thumbed down Ford's invitation was President Wilson's daughter, Margaret. Outstanding members of the clergy also demurred, although sympathetically.

Rabbi Stephen Wise wrote, "While I pray that great good may crown your mission, I would not have such peace as would enthrone ruthless might as arbiter of national destiny . . ."

Ever-controversial Episcopal rector, the Reverend J. Howard Melish, over whom Brooklyn's historic Holy Trinity Church closed its doors, to become, fittingly, the headquarters of the Church Army, put it this way: "The voyage is a symbol . . . it is an embassy of good will. I don't think the trip will accomplish anything, but the trip will create a peace sentiment . . ."

Congregationalist pastor, The Rev. Nehemia Boynton, a leader among clergymen, said, "You know that Don Quixote did not accomplish very much . . . but he went down in history . . . the probabilities are that Mr. Ford will not be the arbiter of the world's peace, but the interests of the trip will be great."

But the laity at large, with no commitment by vocation to charity, put it differently. The Cincinnati economist, Roger Babson, said he'd go if no women were allowed on board. When John Wanamaker said he would go to the end of the earth with Ford, it didn't mean he would go to Europe. William Howard Taft was said to have laughed so hard when he got his invitation that he shook the 23rd Street Ferry. One correspondent reported that the Peace Ship was the idea of a German teacher betrothed to a German officer.

And probably many of the Ford disciples, such as the author of this Ford acrostic, didn't help matters much:

> Hail the apostle of peace
> Eager to have fighting cease
> Nations to lay down their arms
> Return to their cities and farms
> Yuletide to see the War end.
>
> Foe to be turned into friend
> Onward he sails what is banned
> Recruited from all o'er the land
> Daring to lead and we wish him God speed.

The headlong pace was hard on the delegates, too. Mrs. Ada Morse Clark, Secretary to the Chancellor of Stanford, got to New York from her home in California on the eve of sailing. She got a photographer to take her passport photo by flashlight at 11:30 p.m., took the 12:30 to Washington, and at 7 a.m. taxied to the State Army and Navy Building. She persuaded the night watchman to let her in, and phoned the Passport Division Chief. After convincing his butler to wake him up, and then coaxing the official himself to come to the office—he had stayed till midnight the previous night working on Ford party passports—she sent a cab for him. The taxi got lost, and the obliging Passport Chief rode a vegetable truck downtown and filled out Mrs. Clark's passport. By 9 a.m. the hard-breathing lady delegate was back at Union Station, arriving in New York at 2 p.m., one hour before sailing time.

The students' delegation, of which she was to be chaperone, were ultimately to name the assiduous Mrs. Clark "Policeman Clark," and one may perceive what they were up against.

How did Ford weather what already seemed a fiasco? His empire had been built on "Ford jokes," of which two full books were compiled. The Peace Expedition might be considered a colossal Ford joke—the tin lizzie versus Mars. The super-salesman, hopelessly out of his depth, rated it all as having publicity value. That was Ford the businessman.

But the bird-watcher, the husband of a marriage called by his intimate of forty years, Charles E. Sorensen, the most devoted he had ever seen, was all but vanquished by a personal disappointment. His beloved buddy, Thomas Edison, wanted no part of the trip, and this was a blow which Ford could not even bring himself to discuss. To the last minute he had deluded himself that the friend who had accompanied him on their fabled camping trips would be at his side. How sorry we on the ship all felt for Mr. Ford!

"Do you really think it is necessary for me to go along?" Ford actually asked, at the eleventh hour.

Dean Marquis of Detroit's St. Paul Cathedral, believed to move in ways no less mysterious than those of his friend and chief Ford, had brought a letter from Ford's wife: "Now, Henry, you follow the advice of Dr. Marquis. He is discreet and wise."

As to Marquis' application to sail with the delegates, Ford turned the delicate decision over to Mme. Schwimmer. Here the seasoned international diplomat committed what she herself ultimately called her fatal error. Marquis was signed on, among sixty-odd delegates, three newsreel men, thirty-four newsmen, and Ford's personal staff of twenty. Marquis, the "spiritual advisor," who subsequently had to defend scores of "jesuitical" allegations against him, never denied for a moment that his entire motive in joining the Henry Ford Peace Expedition was to sabotage it by detaching its leader at the earliest possible moment. Thus the project was infiltrated at least as mortally as it was beset from without, and the cleric's case held a secret more lethal than any borne by Rosika Schwimmer in her ubiquitous and notorious "little black bag."

As for the Biltmore house-party, long-suffering Louis Lochner recalled it as "an inferno." The Ford clerical staff naturally did not know David Starr Jordan from Joe Smith, and rated the correspondence accordingly. Lochner did not get a vital letter from the prominent Belgian pacifist, Senator Henri La Fontaine, until after the ship had sailed, and one batch of letters reached him two years later. La Fontaine, who received the Nobel Peace Prize in 1913 (the last winner before the holocaust), told me later, when he was a refugee in war-time Paris, how he had expressed horror at the idea of what he called "personal diplomacy," the intervention of busy-bodies—well-meaning or sinister—in the affairs of state, and he cited many historic and contemporary instances where mischief was accomplished by such "meddling."

This theme was embroidered upon by State Department officers during the hectic week, early in December, when the lights were burning in the Passport Bureau, processing the scores of Ford Expedition passports.

"It's a bloody nuisance," was the terse, undiplomatic comment of a deputy assistant secretary of state, whose name is now lost to history. It should be remembered that our State Department was then, and in some ways continues to be, a melange of various hoary practices which our careerists observe overseas and bring back home. An aversion to private meddling in international affairs was one of these.

The foreign service officer, who had done his homework properly, was acutely aware of the Logan Act and how it came to be American law. Dr. George Logan, a Philadelphia Quaker and a leading agronomist of his time was also a member of the Pennsylvania Legislature. At his own expense and initiative he went to France to see Talleyrand about preventing the British from making war. He even discussed his personal mission with Thomas Jefferson and with President Adams and succeeded in staving off hostilities until 1812. But the Federalists resented this "meddling," and they passed the Logan Act of 1799 (Section 953 of the U.S. Code), forbidding a private citizen from undertaking diplomatic negotiations with a foreign power without official authority. The Act went even further and made it illegal for an American citizen to attempt to influence any foreign government or its agents. A fine of $5,000 and a jail sentence of not more than three years is imposed for persons found guilty of private negotiations. The inference drawn from this was that Henry Ford might be hauled off to jail before he ever sailed.

I once heard Lord Balfour say: "In foreign affairs there must be reticence, the business of diplomacy being better done, not by proclaiming our policy at Charing Cross, but by confidential conversations."

My deputy assistant secretary friend went even further: "Even the private kibitzing of monarchs (and spouses of monarchs!) in the foreign affairs of their governments, outside of the control and knowledge of the responsible ministers, has brought about many national disasters. I won't say that Mr. Ford's loony expedition will bring on any disasters, but it could interfere with any genuine peace overtures which might just come from the combatants. In any case, it could jeopardize our neutrality." Like Senator La Fontaine, he likened the ship pilgrims to the irresponsible agents, shady characters, courtiers and all the crude riffraff so well described by the Duke de Broglie in Le Secret du Roi.

Henry Ford wasn't ruffled in the slightest by this kind of comment, much of which was mirrored in editorials across the country. He had already labelled it "poppycock." In a curious way, he found himself in the same boat with one of those "international bankers" he held in so much contempt—the eminent financier Jacob Schiff (grandfather of Dorothy Schiff, publisher of the *New York Post*), who had aroused the ire of the British Cabinet for some *sotto voce* attempts he had made to bring the belligerents together in peace talks. "Ill-timed agitation" and "pro-German peace intrigues" were some of the milder descriptions which came sizzling over the cables from Great Britain.

In any evaluation of the peace-versus-war climate of that period, it must not be overlooked that a profound change had occurred in American thinking since the first year of the war, when the pacifist movement in the United States was, as historian Allan Nevins put it, "not only respectable, but little short of triumphant."

The Lusitania was the *coup de grace* that all the well-intentioned peace makers were being railed against. The "hawks" and the "doves" of World War I had hatched and taken wing. Whenever a rumor of "peace feelers" emanating from the United States was mentioned, Washington felt the need to rush in with avowals of either neutrality or sympathy with the Allied cause. John W. Davis, then Attorney General, used the platform of the Philadelphia Society to assuage the British and to say that "peace proposals at this time would be not only brutal, but impertinent."

On December 12, when the Ford Peace Ship was eight days at sea, the White House put out an official disavowal stating that "President Wilson has neither made suggestions for peace, nor intends to do so in the near future, unless there is an unexpected turn in the belligerent situation." An equally explicit statement followed that same week from the State Department emphatically declaring that the American Ambassador in Berlin, J. W. Gerard, who was on his way back to his post, was positively "not the bearer of any peace proposals." Such declarations were hailed with great satisfaction in Britain showing that President Wilson was "fully alive to the insidious attempts of the enemy to sow discord between the two English-speaking communities."

In a later war, which Ford also opposed (though he threw himself into its prosecution with great vigor), he was to witness several strictly personal and semi-official attempts at private peace-making, such as the flight of Rudolf Hess to Scotland, and the fiasco of the effort by the Duke of Bedford (father of the present one). When it was revealed that the Duke had approached the German Embassy in Dublin to ascertain whether peace pourparlers could be initiated, he was promptly exposed and accused of treason. Actually, the old boy was well-meaning, something of an eccentric "Low Church" pacifist, who greatly exaggerated his social influence and altogether behaved very foolishly.

Before leaving his Biltmore Hotel headquarters for the ship in Hoboken, Ford released an official, detailed Statement of Purpose and Aims, not, of course, written by himself. But his own replies to reporters' questions were characteristic. Standing in the 43rd Street entrance of the hotel, surrounded by a small group of co-workers and a few curious passersby, he shouted, "Tell the people to cry peace and fight preparedness . . . If this expedition fails, I'll start another!" And, getting into his car to drive with Clara and their practical-minded twenty-two-year-old son Edsel, to the pier, he summed it up: "We've got peace-talk going now, and I'll pound it to the end."

The *Boston Traveler*, in far more temperate terms than other segments of the press, saw it this way:

"It is not Mr. Ford's purpose to make peace: he will assemble it."

3

A Backward Look at Pilgrim Ford

Henry Ford was born fifty-one years before his Peace Expedition, as the Civil War raged at its height. It has been suggested by some biographers that he virtually absorbed his later horror of war at his mother's breast. In any case, it is rather noteworthy that no member of the Ford family enlisted.

Ford's birthplace was a Dearborn farm, and its chores were odious to him from earliest boyhood. But a kind of compensatory nostalgia for the whole rural milieu and all the values sentimentally associated with it continued to shape his personal life. He was a teetotaler, and never smoked. The traditional country virtues of loyalty within closely knit family ties, diligence, "get up and git," and clean living in general, always rated high with him. He made something of a cult of simplicity.

"The trouble is," he wrote in his *My Life and Work*, "that the general tendency is to complicate very simple affairs. The farmer makes too complex an affair out of his daily work." The second criterion he listed for the universal car, ranking next

only to quality, is "simplicity in operation—because the masses
are not mechanics." In stating his credo as a manufacturer, he
said, "I thought that it was up to me as the designer to make
the car so completely simple that no one could fail to understand it."

His own book, rather tellingly, is not a biography at all. Was
he so modest, or did he fail to perceive the complex narrative
pattern of human life, even of his own? Actually, it is some
kind of *Confessions of an Industrialist.* Throughout its chapters, certain phrases recur. "Basic logic"—"by the application
of an inevitable principle"—"it could be written down as
a formula"—"anyone can see"—"nobody can deny" and other
banal phrases frame all his accounts of his experiences. Henry
Ford's viewpoint was an arbitrary one. Everything was black
or white. There was no room for nuance, for doubt or for self-
doubt. "Mother," Ford's wife, he also called "the believer," and
it must be inferred that it was himself in whom this belief
chiefly reposed. (Examples of Clara Ford's influence over her
husband, however, as in the matter of the Peace Ship, indicate
that trust did work both ways in this relationship, as in most
close marriages.) Between Ford's simplicity-mystique and his
own unshakable certitude, it is possible to understand his feeling that he could cut most Gordian knots. And he did, except
that of the international holocaust raging in 1915.

As an exponent of simplicity, Ford distrusted experts. He
wrote: "None of our men are 'experts.' We have most unfortunately found it necessary to get rid of a man as soon as he
thinks himself an expert—because no one ever considers him-

Henry Ford. The tintype (upper left) pictures him in fancy clothes
and shoulder length curls at the age of three; (upper right) as a machine shop apprentice at eighteen. In his 40's he wore a jaunty derby
in the 1909 photo (middle left). His office in Highland Park was the
setting for his formal portrait in 1914 (middle right). The next picture is a candid shot taken in 1919, and the final portrait was made
in 1940, when Ford was 77 (lower right). WIDE WORLD PHOTOS.

self expert if he really knows his job." Discounting in theory
the qualifications of experts, Ford could visualize in all serious-
ness his Expedition rushing in triumphant where statesmen
feared to tread. One more ironic touch to the proceedings,
however, is added when we think of Rosika Schwimmer presiding over the venture precisely as "expert advisor." For she was
equipped with all the pretentious trappings, down to the "little
black bag" which she carried everywhere and which was assumed to be full of "secret documents." And the irony is deep-
ened by the charge of some that her self-importance and fond-
ness for mystification helped to undermine the peace mission at
the very start.

Titles were another of Ford's abominations. He believed that
the creation of titles made for red tape and for division of responsibility, to the practical vanishing point of responsibility
itself. He wrote, "Not only is a title often injurious to the
wearer, but it has its effect on others as well. There is perhaps
no greater single source of personal dissatisfaction among men
than the fact that the title-bearers are not always the real leaders." His cavalier treatment of President Wilson, as we saw,
bears out Ford's deprecation of titles.

Ford deplores in his memoir the waste, inefficiency, and
needlessly hard work of the farm-life of his early youth. He
notes, rather in passing, the conflict with his father. The elder
Ford wanted Henry to keep on with the farm. But the son was
infatuated with mechanics and rebelled at the drudgery of
farming. It would seem that certain tensions the situation generated in Henry Ford remained unresolved. With his own son,
Edsel, he reduplicated, almost as if in a misdirected vengeance,
his own father's insistence on the heir's following in the pater-
nal footsteps. However, Edsel was a man of an entirely different
breed, a college man who adhered strictly to the business of
automobile making.

But Henry Ford often seemed to try to relive the old farmlife
days, as when he made a great project of reviving the old coun-

try dances. This was one of many instances when Ford made it hard for people to keep up with him, in this case, invited guests in his home. Done up in painstakingly authentic period costume, Ford would have his company, who in that era would have been happier in the charleston, or at least the fox trot, sashaying and do-se-do-ing, as if he believed he could bring another America back to life.

His lack of letters apparently remained a sensitive point with Ford. At the country school house, he had had a routine primary education which, it is certain, did not fire his intellect. The boyhood achievement he relates with the greatest pride is constructing a watch with two dials to keep daylight and standard time. But even in his mechanical tinkering he showed no inventive genius superior to that of many other boys of his time, when machinery was as enormous a revelation as space-science is today. Rather he had dogged persistence, which seems owed in part to pure blindness to many other elements of experience, single-mindedness in pursuit of one sound idea. One idea, Ford rightly saw, was all it takes. A car for the average person (Ford hated the word *standardized*) was the touchstone of his success. He was not, like his idol, Thomas Edison, a really creative mind.

Repeatedly, Ford disparaged formal education, even "knowledge." He said that one may become "an overloaded factbox," that "great piles of knowledge in the head" do not necessarily stimulate thought, that "fashions in knowledge" make its acquisition a very relative affair. Even for himself, Ford's flat statements on "knowledge" are especially arbitrary. "The only reason why every man does not know everything that the human mind has ever learned is that no one has ever yet found it worth while to know that much." "One good way to hinder progress is to fill a man's head with all the learning of the past . . . merely gathering knowledge may become the most useless work a man can do." These oversimplifications, the contempt for history ("history is bunk"), and the lack of recognition of any relation between event and evaluation, between datum and thought, we meet with overwhelmingly in the Peace crusade. It has been likened, in fact, to the Children's Crusade of the naive Middle Ages.

In the old truism of many a "self-made" man, Ford declared that you learn more from life than you learn from books. More interesting than the arrogance with which he imparts that learning is the frequent graciousness with which we find Ford accepting it.

Ford hero-worshipped Thomas Edison from the age of twenty-five or so. It was to Edison that the young Henry confided his concept of the light-weight, high horsepowered, self-contained engine. "His (Edison's) knowledge is almost universal . . . he recognizes no limitations. He believes that all things are possible. At the same time he keeps his feet on the ground." It is easy to appreciate Ford's disappointment that Edison kept his feet on the ground when all the other believers that all things are possible were boarding the Oscar II.

Forming a trio with Edison and Ford was John Burroughs, and it was with Burroughs that Ford pursued his housing-for-birds project. Ford's bird-hotel, the Ponchartrain, boasted seventy-six apartments. But just as Ford demanded high personal standards of his employees, he was critical of his birds. "Sparrows," he stated severely, "are great abusers of hospitality." In spite of his passion for the indigenously American, he was driven by the abusive sparrows to exotic birds. He imported five hundred from Europe—larks, chaffinches, red pales, yellow-hammers. "Birds are the best of companions," he wrote. "We need them for their beauty and companionship, and also we need them for the strictly economic reason that they destroy harmful insects." Beauty, companionship, and "the strictly economic" are not dichotomous to Ford's mind. But ill-fated, as so many of Ford's personal hobbies and caprices were, the "best of companions" soon parted company with their importer. The rare birds inhabited the Ford bird-hotels briefly, and then vanished. Quietly, as always, in a mood of chagrin, Ford recorded simply, "I shall not import any more. Birds are entitled to live where they want to live."

Misfortune seems to have haunted everything Ford did that was not for personal gain. A more tragic case in point was that of his sending an old friend's son to study his chosen field, forestry. En route to the work site, the boy fell from the wagon under its wheels and was crushed to death. Ford's comment here was, "In his college they didn't teach him how to sit on the wagon."

Another irony, in the light of Ford's supercilious attitude toward formal learning, was the deep entrenchment with him, for a number of years, of Dean Marquis. One of the Peace Ship voyagers, the intellectual Dean was its acknowledged saboteur. Whatever else Marquis perpetrated, it is perhaps most poignant to think of Ford at the mercy—especially when seasick —of the art-loving, opera-going, literary doctor of theology. Exposure to concentrated culture seems to have been more than enervating to Ford; it was virtually lethal. And this was to be his personal fate on his Expedition.

At the turn of his half-century mark, Henry Ford's career was at its zenith. The year 1915—the year of the Peace Ship —was the climax and turning point for him. Although his fortune, compared to what it would eventually become, was modest, he had certainly far more money than a man knew what to do with. In fact, like a Henry James hero, Ford was possessed of total moral freedom. His power of choice was uninhibited by any practical exigency.

We may recall that it was always in these aesthetically perfect circumstances that James' heroes or heroines got themselves into, or were gotten into by others, their worst trouble. In personality, too, Ford reminds us of one of James' "Americans" of this period—i.e. innocent, simple, naive, outspoken, yet with a certain canniness. Having done everything there was to be done at home, he sets out on the ultimate venture, to de-

May 16 -34

RECEIVED
MAY 17 1934

Hello Old Pal:-

Arrived here at 10 A.M. today.
Would like to drop in and see you...
You have a wonderful car. Been driving
it for three weeks. It's a treat to drive one.
Your slogan should be,
Drive a Ford and watch the other cars
fall behind you. I can make any other
car take a Ford's dust.

Bye — Bye.

John Dillinger

John Dillinger's letter, praising the Model "T" as a "get-away car."

cadent, mysterious, omniscient, predatory Europe. And the volatile moral adventuress, as Ford's elite guard saw Mme. Schwimmer, makes a perfect foil.

Ford, whose life now at early middle age was little more than half over, gave a dainty, almost frail impression physically. The man of action and ambition, who could not let go of his single idea till it was executed, whose criterion for a college was an "intellectual gymnasium," appeared burned down to nerve. Sorensen relates that when Ford was visited by President and Mrs. Franklin Roosevelt during World War II, the tycoon was almost camouflaged by the ample Roosevelts who flanked him on either side.

There is a fascinating little optical-illusory trick which may be played with one of Ford's portrait-photographs. If one side of Ford's face is covered, a benign, gently humorous expression dominates. When the other side is covered, the look is transformed into one of deadly, malevolent calculation. This ambiguous effect is created by Ford's hollow, heavy-lidded eyes, the pale eyes one would associate with either a visionary or a killer. In his dress Ford was at the same time sartorially formal and rather homely. His custom finery was apt to be a bit worn.

The self-made man, in 1915, was certainly *made*. All his unique achievements in his primary role had been accomplished. He had built the model T—and it is seldom now thought of that this historic vehicle bears its name quite arbitrarily by virtue of its nineteen predecessors. It was not a fortuity, but Ford's sedulous calculation. It revolutionized American society—it put America on the road.

Another revolution, an economic one, was realized. This was the $5-day. This milestone in industry occurred a little more than a year before the Peace Expedition—on January 14, 1914. It was the result of the rounding-off of a detailed algebraic analysis. This was the equation of materials, overhead, and labor based on expanding production, lowered car prices, and rising profits. All this was computed to the last penny on the blackboard in Ford's office. The $5-wage figure, evened from an exact $4.78, was fully absorbed by savings from lower costs, higher production, and more efficient production facilities, not to mention tremendously increased labor incentive. And it was about twice the standard wage at that time.

This was the crowning event of the most progressive Ford Company period, 1914–19. It was front-page news from coast to coast and even made headlines abroad. Ford was hailed as a great human benefactor, and damned as a socialist. It was actually, of course, simply sound business. And the value of the publicity accruing from it was immeasurable. Fifty million dollars worth of free advertising was one assessment of the move, which Ford called not charity, but "profit-sharing and efficiency engineering," radical concepts for that era.

This was also the period when the River Rouge project was fermenting in Ford's mind; it was likewise the start of what was to become the "sociological department" of the plant, later headed by Dean Marquis. All of this was, to Ford, just "good business." In his book he decried paternalism. Yet at the same time he categorized his employees in three classes:

1. Married men living with and taking good care of their families.
2. Single men over twenty-two years of age who are of proved thrifty habits.
3. Young men under twenty-two years of age, and women who are the sole support of some next of kin.

For some of these factors to be objectively determined presupposes a real espionage system. Ford also remarked casually, "We had to break up the evil custom among many of the foreign workers of taking in boarders—of regarding their homes as something to make money out of rather than as a place to live in." Simultaneously, he said, "Single men who lived wholesomely shared (the profit-sharing plan)," and "There are objections to the bonus-on-conduct method of paying wages. It tends toward paternalism. Paternalism has no place in industry. Welfare work that consists of prying into employees' private concerns is out of date."

The explosion of publicity set off by the inauguration of the $5-day not only changed the face of the American industrial scene; publicity and power wrought changes in Henry Ford.

Or, at any rate, being cast into such focus demanded a kind of codification process. In this we watch the man who loved machines entangle himself deeper and deeper in his own rationalizations.

The year of the Peace Expedition also marked the close of the first Ford era with respect to his elite guard, which configured personalities as controversial and thoroughly scandalized by sinister rumors as the great man himself. There was James Couzens, the financial head known for his knack for squeezing a dollar harder than anybody else. Nevertheless, Couzens went along with, possibly even devised, the $5-day, because it augmented his personal publicity for the political career he sought before Ford ever got into that arena.

In October Couzens resigned, although he stayed on as a director. For each of them, the other had served his purpose. It was Ford's hardening pacifism that sparked the final blow-up between them. With Couzens out of the way, for all practical purposes, Ford no doubt started really feeling his oats at last. From the zenith attained around 1915, Ford was to go off on more and more tangents. For a man of his temperament and narrow capacities, there actually was nowhere else to go. The Peace Ship was the first of such wild flights.

"A fool and his flivver are soon carted" was one of the more succinct of the "Ford jokes" of the time, which really seem in that period to have outnumbered jokes about death or sex. Ford had something of his own to say about fools, in the light of which we cannot but think of his "ship of fools:"

"There is . . . the great fear of being thought a fool. So many men are afraid of being considered fools. I grant that public opinion is a powerful police influence for those who need it. Perhaps it is true that the majority of men need the restraint of public opinion. Public opinion may keep a man better than he would otherwise be—if not better morally, at least better as far as his social desirability is concerned. But it is not a bad thing to be a fool for righteousness' sake. The best of it is that such fools usually live long enough to prove that they were no fools—or the work they have begun lives long enough to prove they were not foolish."

4

Pacifist Syndrome-Circa 1915

Against the lurid backdrop of mortar shellings and ship-sinkings of the Great War, there was a dramatic confrontation at home. As always tends to happen under conditions of conflict, every extremity rises to the fore. The serious and subtle minds, too sensitive spontaneously to absorb the impact of shock, recoil in bemusement. The lunatic fringes move to center stage. All the valid nuances of significant concepts are blotted out to black and white. It is an atmosphere in which responsible thought languishes beside sweeping oversimplifications.

Around 1915, the confrontation was between "milkfaced grubs" and "bloody-minded militarists." The philosophical question agreed was "Would you fight if a foreign soldier struck your mother?" The July 29, 1915 issue of LIFE magazine (the old comic weekly) depicted William Jennings Bryan with a peacock tail, proclaiming:

> I want to be a neutral,
>   And with the neutrals stand,
> A smile upon my ego,
>   The German vote at hand.

Other cartoons showed him leaving the Cabinet with a white feather in his hat. A German cartoon showed pacifists trying to bury the hatchet of war in an ink pot. And the time did indeed seem gone in which the pen was mightier than the sword.

In this total exploitation of the whole idea of peace, this general vulgarization, the movement was traduced. The more to be marvelled at is the staunchness of those absolute pacifists who weathered the extreme climate of the confrontation.

Within the pacifist camp itself, feeling was much divided. The basic conflict was between the "preparedness" and "no preparedness" camps—not to mention the "no preparedness for *this* war" element, which was pro-German. This last poses another problem, bringing us up to the current identification of many pacifist groups with the "Red-tainted," the "subversives." A catalogue of "Friends of Peace" in 1915 read much like a list of nationalist societies. There was the German-American Alliance, the United Irish Societies, the American Truth Society, the American Women of German Descent, the German-American Peace Society, the American Humanity League.

This proliferation of obviously far from disinterested peace groups posed another deep problem for true pacifists. Yet, in all fairness to all "bloody-minded militarists," it must be noted that pacifists often seem to be such because they recognize such a militant spirit in themselves. Many a "fighting pacifist" evidences a violence of feeling alarming to those believers in the occasional validation of war who, themselves, could not hurt a fly.

Simultaneous with the whole peace movement, relief and aid societies were cropping up wildly, many bearing very graphic names. There was the War Babies' Cradle, the American Red Star Animal Relief, the American Committee for Training Soldiers in Suitable Trades, the Maimed Soldiers of France, and many others of similarly explicit purposes, so that a sympathizer wishing to specialize was offered a wide range of

choices. Enrico Caruso had his American Committee in Aid of Italian Refugees and Soldiers Crippled in War, and Otto Kahn, August Belmont, and Vincent Astor had their Permanent Blind Relief War Fund.

Against this chaotic moral scene, it was the onerous responsibility of President Wilson to delineate this new American self-consciousness, this new image of the American self which was being forged in the fires at home no less than those raging abroad.

In his address to a meeting of the Associated Press in New York on April 20, 1915, Wilson, one of the most literate of our Presidents, seemed to arrive at some perspective from which to promulgate a kind of "authorized version."

"We are the mediating Nation of the world. I do not mean that we undertake not to mind our own business and to mediate where other people are quarreling. I mean the word in a broader sense. We are compounded of the nations of the world; we mediate their blood, we mediate their traditions, we mediate their sentiments, their tastes, their passions; we are ourselves compounded of those things. We are, therefore, able to understand all nations . . . not separately, as partisans, but unitedly as knowing and comprehending and embodying them all . . . America . . . is ready to turn, and free to turn, in any direction . . . The United States has no racial momentum. It has no history . . . which makes it run . . . in one particular direction. And America is particularly free in this, that she has no hampering ambitions as a world power."

And more, in the same address was kin to Henry Ford's "small man:"

". . . I am interested in neutrality because there is something so much greater to do than fight; there is a distinction waiting for this Nation that no nation has ever yet got . . . The distinction of absolute self-control and self-mastery . . . I covet for America this splendid courage of reserve moral force . . ."

Then, further on, Wilson outlined the Ford concept of the man "too right to fight:"

"The example of America must be the example not merely of peace because it will not fight, but of peace because peace is the healing and elevating influence of the world and strife is not. There is such a thing as a man being too proud to fight. There is such a thing as a nation being so right that it does not need to convince others by force that it is right."

Obviously, this brilliant enunciation of an "official version," the more to be wondered at when we think of the bombastic prose usual in those times, did not come forth out of the blue. The idealism expressed in Wilson's uniquely powerful imagery had a distinguished tradition behind it.

Before we examine this tradition, it should be noted that at the same time that the impact of the Great War fractionalized pacific thinking, it disciplined and codified it. The shock of the war was at least as stunning to people in those days as that of nuclear weapons in ours. We have no recorded examples of people igniting their bodies or fasting unto death in protest against war. But we do know that such figures as the young Bertrand Russell and George Trevelyan expressed, in terms of which one can hardly doubt the sincerity, the desire to die.

Henry James, who at this time rapidly failed and sank to his death, whose whole literary metier had been the juxtaposition of pristine America and tragic, prostituted Europe, said: "To have to take it for what all the years were making for, and meaning, is too tragic for any words." (Too tragic, of course, for any words but those of James.)

This sense of betrayal by life itself, by history, by mankind, is the strongest reaction we meet from the personalities of real sensibility of the epoch. E. M. Forster, the great English novelist, wrote "the modern Europe . . . should fall into the Devil's trap . . ."

British-descended Jack London told the press, "I am with the Allies life and death." His view of Germany was hardly less impassioned than Owen Wister's "Germany today is a paranoiac . . . never before in history has a whole nation gone insane."

Closely linked with many of these commentators is London's one line evaluation of the war: "The World War has been a pentecostal cleansing of the spirit of man."

The "Safety Firsters" in America infuriated Jack London, and it is said that the execution of English nurse Edith Cavell on espionage charges brought him to a state of frenzy which lasted for days. As for Belgium, when the English religious novelist Hal Caine, whose works were then appearing on Broadway and on the silent screen, asked Jack London to contribute to *The King Albert Book,* a testimonial to Belgian heroism, London's response was one of the most fervent.

"Among men arises on rare occasions a great man, a man of cosmic import or a great nation . . . Such a nation is Belgium.

Such is the place Belgium attained in a day by one mad, magnificent, heroic leap into the azure. As long as the world rolls and men live, that long will Belgium be remembered."

Here is the way "improper" pacifist Emily Balch put it: "At first the war seemed almost incredible." Her refusal to accept the idea of war was, as a matter of fact, to shape both her own long life and much of that of the whole peace movement. Her name and honors have prominently been recalled in Fiftieth Anniversary commemoration in 1965 of the Women's International League for Peace and Freedom. Immediately after World War I, Miss Balch joined the editorial staff of the *Nation* on one of Oswald Garrison Villard's sections. In 1946 she was awarded the Nobel Peace Prize. Her "Letter to China" of 1955, six years before her death at the age of ninety-four, concludes with the line, "Groping, we may find one another's hands in the dark." Her friend, Jane Addams, famous for Chicago's Hull House, and herself the Nobel Peace Prize winner for 1931, summed it up:

"It is impossible now to reproduce that basic sense of desolation, of suicide, of anachronism, which that first news of the war brought to thousands of men and women who had come to consider war as a throwback in the scientific sense."

It should be borne in mind that, although the international picture was different between wars when these pacifist leaders were voicing such judicious reflections, the most impressive thing about them was their consistency—an exercise in straight-line pugnacity about peace covering fifty years. They are set down and capsuled in this narrative of the Peace Ship only to establish the climate and set the mood in which the Ford Expedition was conceived. The frustrations and conflicting interests which were at the root of the conflict were certainly not fully understood one year after the outbreak of World War I, and the loud noises which burst from many throats came in a torrential chorus only after months of tongue-tied impotency. The rabbit had been staring mutely into the face of the cobra, then suddenly jumped, first with a snarl, then a loud snort.

If one had listened in on some of the heated discussions which permeated the campuses of the larger universities, one would have found the counterpart of a latter-day "teach-in," infinitely smaller in student involvement, to be sure, but, none-theless, passionate and militant.

Off-campus these same young men would gather in the "red-ink joints"—tiny Italian restaurants in Greenwich Village, where the red wine was included in the 50¢ *table d'hote*—or, in tea-rooms (not yet coffee houses) like Romany Marie's. There such young radicals as Frank Tannenbaum (now an aging professor, head of the Latin American Department at Columbia University), the late Joseph Freeman, leader of the debating society at New York University, a novelist who was later read out of the U.S. Communist party as a "romantic," were joined around the table by talkers like Maxwell Boden-heim, Harry Kemp, George Sokolsky and their young cohorts. "The boy" who wasn't "raised to be a soldier," Frank Tannen-baum, was spouting the anti-war credo and also fully con-curred in the sentiment around his soap-box. The talk, cap-suled and paraphrased, as far as a non-participant can recall, went something like this:

"The Nineteenth century is over! It died slowly, but it's over forever. This is the end of our isolation."

"The big mistake we've made, as I see it," said a youngster who later taught history at City College in New York, "is our interpretation of history. Up to now, we believed history re-vealed aspirations approaching fulfillment. Our attitude to the world has been, look what *we've* done, and you do likewise."

"The thing I fear," said another, "is this state of nerves we're in. This present war, because of its magnitude and nearness, has got us in a state of morbid excitement."

"Oh, in Europe they're always having a war!" had been the American attitude before 1915. Of course, they were thinking of the Balkan wars. "We believe in minding our own business

and staying out of their quarrels. We don't want anything
that's not ours, and we're not getting fixed to fight. Of course, if
somebody was so crazy as to try to take anything away from us,
we'd go for the shotgun!"

"That's better than being dead, being smug and provincial.
We've been shaken up. Our ideas are in flux. People are thinking. This is healthy."

"But *how* are people thinking? As if all the future was going
to be one continuing cataclysm! We say we hate the war, but
we're identifying with the war, we're taking on the mental
quality of those Europeans in the trenches."

"We've still got a choice, as I see it," from another table-
talker, "We've still got that latitude. All right, we've become
part of the rest of the world. But on what terms? For good or
for ill? Are we going in to fight for the spoils or to fight for
peace?"

"But we haven't got the basic prerequisite to theorize ration-
ally on war *or* peace! Americans believe that one man started
all this. As long as people hang onto the villain theory of history, there's no motivation, no destiny."

"I'll tell you the thing I fear. It's our tepid, cornfed idealism,
driving a Ford to church and writing a check for Belgium or
China, all lackluster good will."

"That same cornfed idealism freed the slaves. What worries
me is the crude picture that's been stamped on our minds. It's
prejudice and fear that are going to determine us; whether we
arm, against *whom* we arm. Everything we've cared for all
along is out the window. We're over-reacting to everything.
We've got to be *active*. We don't want war, but we want to
measure up to the standards of war. That's all that matters to
people now. And they're acting as if nothing else ever will
again."

They were philosophers—most of these young men of 1915
—and, unlike their inflammatory counterparts of the 1960's,
there was no parroting of words and ideas which originated on

UP IN THE CLOUDS —Kirby in N. Y. *World*

television panel shows, or in radio news analysis.

Although an ocean still lay between, in the tremor of the musketry, shells and artillery of Europe, America was, as would be said fifty years later, "All shook up."

"Preparedness" advocates and pacifists alike were up against intense American provincialism. This is present in every attitude of Ford's which we have noted. The jolt of the war threw Ford, like many anonymous people (and his birds), out of the nest. In their noblest efforts to fly, it dashed them to earth. A great measure of Ford's personal tragedy was this. He inadvertently, through the fortuity of his wealth, his fame, polarized in himself both elements. He was an American farm boy, aspiring beyond the farm, but still loving above everything else "to run and jump fences;" who, by virtue of the Jamesian moral freedom of enough money to do anything, including charter a steamship, found himself deeply involved with all the celebrated bluestockings of the time, with those who had studied at the feet of the sage of Yasnaya Polyana, the fabled Tolstoi estate, and lived with the Masaryk family in Prague, and with the professional, dilettante, liberal, free-thinking, banner-carrying dissidents of the moment.

Compare their utterances with Ford's: *"It was war that made the orderly and profitable processes of the world what they are today—a loose, disjointed mass . . . Business should be on the side of peace, because peace is business' best asset. And was inventive genius ever so sterile as it was during war?"*

Phoenixlike, pacifist thought rose from its ashes and its sackcloth. It reassembled itself along clearer and more decisive lines than ever in the motley history of the movement. But this decisiveness was also divisive.

One may distinguish two mainstreams of significant pacifism at this time. Both have in common an international heritage. America, like its Jamesian protagonist, like Henry Ford himself, was not strong on original philosophy. The thinker has to "keep quiet and be still." America's tradition was all action and "westering."

The recognized sages were Europeans. Pilgrimages to the shrine of the giant among them, the prophet-author of *War and Peace*, Count Leo Tolstoi, were still being made. Jane Addams, especially, worshipped at this altar of the aged Russian saint.

A seasoned and mature European culture was the backbone of both chief pacifist trends. One was absolutely religious in basis. These literal Christians adhered to the "suffering servant" concept of the messianic message of Isaiah, fulfilled for them in the witness of Jesus Christ "extending His arms of love at all times to all nations."

The other, more heterogeneous in character, and far more dominant, gathered together those members of the international-feminist-suffragist-pacifist schools. A kind of counter-chauvinism, such as we see in extreme form in the Black Nationalists of today, seems to have imbued these women with a belief in the moral superiority of women. By their nature, presumably, women would inevitably always vote for peace and against war. Hence, the identity of their peace movement with the vote for women.

Both groups, or their direct heirs, continue to dominate the peace movement in our own day.

The religious pacifists consolidated a few months after the start of the Great War in Cambridge, England, in December, 1914. Christened the Fellowship of Reconciliation, and still functioning actively as such today, it was (and is) interdenominational. But it was united in the belief that Christians are forbidden to support any war in any way. They are committed to the way of "Love" in all dealings, both personal and extra-personal; and to the offering of themselves "for God's redemptive purposes," in whatever form these may be revealed. (Obvious present-day descendants are the various nonviolent groups.)

A year later, three weeks before the launching of Ford's Peace Ship, the F.O.R. was established in the United States at Garden City, the Episcopal cathedral-city of Long Island.

The F.O.R. readiness for martyrdom, in whatever sense it might befall, was soon tested and not found wanting. An Episcopal rector of Cincinnati was literally tarred, feathered, horse-whipped and ridden out of town on a rail. Only fast and inspired action by a local lawyer prevented identical treatment being meted out to no less a personage than Bishop Paul Jones of Salt Lake City.

It is interesting that no proponents of peace seemed to goad the war-minded segments of the public so ferociously as the religious, as if the militarists themselves felt a call to impersonate T. S. Eliot's Fourth Tempter—that to martyrdom.

In any case, many F.O.R. members achieved, if only, as in

Bishop Jones' case, through deprivation of their position, the self-offering they believed in. In this they won a certain moral victory over the secular pacifists.

5

Flesh and Blood Doves of Peace

The women's peace crusaders had as their irresistible selling point, then and now, the spectacle of "the mess *men* have made of things."

It was an unarguable point and every man and woman in the street could grasp it. This included my non-political mother, a professional violinist before she married my father, a sculptor who put his talents to the design and manufacture of lamps and art objects. Mother bore six children—two boys and four girls—and, although I am the eldest, at the time of the Peace Ship sailing, I was but her teenage son who was getting involved, perhaps perilously, in a war and peace mission.

I saved the letters she wrote to me during this time, as she did mine. This particular one surprised me for all its political remarks and zealous feminism, for my Ma would much rather be baking a cake or listening to music than getting all excited about world problems.

Dear Son:

How are you? I worry, I can't help it. You read such terrible things every day, but I'm glad you should have such an opportunity. It's an education.

Pop brought the papers home and to read them was a disgrace. People have no respect. I'll tell you what it is. Mark my words. It's the men! They say to have a woman on board is bad luck, but this time it's the men. On the Noordam, did anybody laugh because it was all women? In a war, who suffers? Men don't suffer. To them it's adventure. It's women who suffer. They say Mr. Ford made his big mistake when he took up with Mrs. Schwimmer. Well, I say the peace women made their big mistake when they took up with *men*.

Women are born pacifists. I said it to Pop and what he replied I wouldn't write.

Last year when the Noordam sailed, their flag was homemade. They didn't need a million dollars. People had respect, it was kept decent. Pop looked at the papers from Hoboken and said to me: Your son's joined the circus. He works on a newspaper and that's what happens. He should have gotten a job. I could have fixed it for him to become an ashtray designer.

But I tell you another thing, people can't forget the Lusitania. And it was a terrible thing, all those people. But people are extreme. Already they say to me, your son's on the Oscar—he's pro-German?

Nowadays everything is pro and anti. The most peaceful people you ever saw, who wouldn't hurt a fly themselves. And a funny thing, a lot of times it's the pacifists who are at each other's throats. But it's like a disease. Everybody is a hothead now, to go in or to stay out. In the book you have by Owen Wister, he says it will take a calamity of the whole world for them to learn, so he wants a calamity. And the boys you knew at Columbia, they say it's all Capital, but on Belgium they have other opinions. Now Jack London leaving the Socialist Party didn't surprise me. Of him I'd expect anything.

But mark my words. Some day the countries will have to get together. Maybe they'll only get together to fight some more, but there will be something. Maybe this could be the beginning, if they listen mostly to the women. I'm glad you went, I'm very glad, only I worry, with the sinkings and the spies in the papers. Dress warm. I packed a honey cake inside your clean socks. Eat it, it won't keep forever.

The girls keep asking, when will you get back. Pop talks about you to all his big business friends. Always I'm thinking about you, and miss you.

Ma

The Noordam mentioned in mother's letter was the name of a Dutch vessel, the *first* peace ship which had sailed from Hoboken,—the New Jersey port later to be travestied—on April 13, 1915, only eight months earlier than its successor, Oscar II. Excluding the captain and sailors, there wasn't a man aboard the ship except women. The feminine touch was noticeable even in the ship's gently-flowing hand-made banner inscribed simply, "PEACE."

On this voyage, in contrast to Ford's Expedition, there was no horseplay.

Yes, the women had done it before, on another ship, with another congress, and another delegation. At a time when leading men pacifists—called "Molly Coddles"—such as those who supported the Carnegie Endowment for International Peace, were squashed into retreat ("This is no time to talk peace; we shall make ourselves ridiculous"), it was the women who rose above the fear of making themselves ridiculous and formed the passenger list for the Noordam.

Insight into the dangers inherent in such a mission is perceptibly recorded in the diary of Emily Balch. "We are a very heterogeneous group of mostly highly individualized women used to being leaders and playing a conspicuous role, 'rebels' by temperament . . . no one knows what it is sensible to attempt or to leave undone. As a consequence there is naturally some nervous tension, a lack of cohesion, a tendency to criticize and to suspect the authorities and pull apart . . . I think we are trying to prevent such a tendency gaining on us . . ." Later, she summed up: "These days together have . . . welded us together . . . we do not suppose we have power or knowledge or importance. We just mean to do what we can . . ."

This self-effacing assessment of the situation is in diametrical contrast to that of Henry Ford in his telegraphed invitation to his own Expedition: "The time has come for a few men and women with courage and energy . . . to free the goodwill of Europe that it may assert itself for peace and justice, with the strong probability that international disarmament can be accomplished."

The ladies of the first peace overtures to Europe were sailing for The Hague International Congress of Women; this was to be followed up by delegations to the war capitals, to the northern capitals, and finally to the United States—which was to lead eventually to Henry Ford's meeting with the crusading Rosika Schwimmer. Theodore Roosevelt, characterized by the women pacifists as a militant "Red Blood," condemned the Noordam voyage as "silly and base."

Owen Wister, a bestselling novelist of the period and author of "The Pentecost of Calamity," published in 1915, was far more deprecating of the peace seekers than the man who carried the big stick. Wister proclaimed "righteous war" as the "finding of one's own soul." Writing of heroes who had left behind war widows, he said: "And what do the women say—the women who lose such men? Thus do they decline to attend at The Hague the Peace Congress of foolish women who have lost

nobody . . ." In an outburst of a kind of militant vampirism,
Wister quotes:

> End Europe so? Then, in Thy Mercy, God,
> Out of the foundering planet's gruesome night
> Pluck Thou my people's soul.

It was against this fever pitch, no less than against the war
itself that both the Noordam voyage and the Oscar II expedi-
tions were pitted. But the all-woman approach and the Henry
Ford approach were different.

On the eve of her embarkation on the Noordam, Jane Addams wrote: "We do not think we can settle the war. We do
not think that by raising our hands we can make the armies
cease slaughter. We do think it is valuable to state a new point
of view. We do think it is fitting that women should meet and
take counsel to see what may be done."

And her friend pacifist, Emily Balch, thirty years after the
sailing, when she was seventy-nine, retrospectively quoted
Emily Dickinson:

> I aimed my pebble, but myself
> Was all the one that fell.
> Was it Goliath was too large,
> Or only I too small?

On his own Peace Ship, the super-confident Ford had declared: "I'll bet this ship against a penny that we'll have the
boys out of the trenches by Christmas. I'll buy the Oscar II as a
souvenir if we succeed."

If Rosika Schwimmer fell into controversy and was less than
a brilliant success as a policy maker and negotiator of the Ford
Peace Expedition, quite the opposite had been true of her celebrated career and reputation as a world patriot until then. She
was known to have uncanny perception and judgment; to be
an effective suffrage and peace leader; a most competent journalist; an extremely interesting lecturer; a social worker who

fought for child welfare programs.

In 1914, Mme. Schwimmer lived in London as a correspondent for a string of top European newspapers and served with distinction as International Press Secretary of the International Women's Suffrage Alliance. An example of her stature and talent for never underestimating the calamity of the times may be drawn from her memorable visit, on July 9, 1914, with David Lloyd George at 11 Downing Street.

Rosika had followed closely a series of international incidents culminating in the assassination of the Austrian Archduke. At the meeting with the British Prime Minister, she warned him: "We are taking the assassination much too quietly. It has provoked a storm throughout the Austrian Empire as I have never witnessed. Unless something is done immediately to satisfy resentment, I think it can result in war with Serbia, with the horrible consequences this might precipitate all over Europe!"

Lloyd George noted in his *War Memoirs* that official reports did not seem to justify the alarmist view she took, but a few weeks later she was proved correct, and he credited Mme. Schwimmer with being "the only person I met at the time who was aware of the imminence of world conflict."

From the day war was declared, and considerably before her alignment with Ford, Rosika Schwimmer never tired of distributing her Continuous Mediation peace appeal which began: "To All Men, Women, and Organizations who want to stop international massacre at the earliest possible moment . . ." The appeal outlined a plan for continuous mediation to the belligerent governments by the United States and the neutrals: Switzerland, Netherlands, Sweden, Denmark, Norway and Spain. It was translated into every needed language and circulated internationally. The encouraging response came in cabled endorsements from outstanding organizations across the globe, so that, in September, Rosika was able to arrive in the

United States bearing impressive international sanction of her plan.

Her colleague and traveling companion was Mrs. Carrie Chapman Catt, with whom she interviewed Secretary of State Bryan. But the big day came on September 18, 1914, when Mme. Schwimmer presented to President Wilson at the White House the International Petition which urged him to call a Neutral Conference for Continuous Mediation. He was cordial and sympathetic, and noncommittal.

To put the pressure of public opinion upon the President for an affirmative decision, she made a lecture tour of 22 states, arousing thousands to write Wilson to call a Neutral Conference. Her most effective cry was: "If you do not help us end the war in Europe before the militarists end it, you too will be drawn in!"

Rosika's tour resulted in the birth of the Woman's Peace Party, with Jane Addams, President, and herself, International Secretary. She also inspired the formation of the Emergency Peace Federation in Chicago (December 19, 1914), which adopted her plan for a Neutral Conference based on Continuous Mediation, at the time she was deeply immersed in the Ford Peace mission. The EPF also called for the establishment of a world peace organization and outlined terms of post-war settlement later embodied in Wilson's "Fourteen Points," and later, the ill-fated League of Nations, and today's United Nations.

Rosika Schwimmer was unique in employing her then new technique of using the resolutions and plans she authored as tools of personal liaison by which she went on to achieve the action proposed. She was a people-to-people doer. Her deeds never died on paper but went on to implementation, sometimes was lasting success, sometimes not, but always with some definite positive gain, even in the case of the ill-fated Ford Peace Expedition. More and more historians are describing the Expedition and Rosika's leadership in it as the first democratic attempt on the part of the people to end the war before military victory could be achieved, and the first to start a new world order which would bar violence from the settlement of human dispute.

As the Noordam headed for the Hague International Congress of Peace, Rosika urged and convinced Jane Addams to accept the burden of presiding over the 2,000 distinguished women from belligerent and neutral countries assembled at the Congress. It lasted from April 28 to May 1, 1915 and was known popularly as "The Palace of Doves."

With Jane Addams at the helm, Rosika's own contributions came, as usual, in the form of creative paper work. In her most important resolution, proposed, seconded by Julia Grace Wales and accepted, she convinced the Congress that its own delegates should carry the resolutions to the belligerent and neutral governments. "We must have face-to-face meetings to urge their acceptance," she said. Rosika drew much of her backing from the gifted initiator of the Congress, Dr. Aletta Jacobs, a Dutch physician and well-known suffragette.

It may not have been very politic of the ladies to have allowed Miss Wales the honor of seconding Rosika's resolution, for the intrusion of Julia's strange personality into these serious settings might have been fodder for the newsmen, and might have doomed the resolution as a "farce."

Julia, to put it in modern terms, was known as a "kookie seer," and, in psychiatric circles, as a disturbed, but harmless, hallucinatory spiritualist.

The young Canadian-born Julia taught English at the University of Wisconsin, but often went into solo seances, in and outside the classroom, identifying herself with Joan of Arc. In one of her "visions," she had perceived that "the neutrals should gather in Switzerland, that there they should 'sit,' perpetually dedicated to evaluating day-by-day events toward the pinpointing of ways to 'tempt' the belligerents to peace." This

"vision," which she spoke of loud and clear, linked her to the women's peace movement in the United States and abroad, and this is how she came to her alliance with the more down-to-earth proponent of Continuous Mediation, Rosika Schwimmer.

There was no rivalry between the two women; neither was power mad, and it was generally known that Rosika's "earth vision" had come along considerably before Julia's "heavenly guidance." The harmony between the women and the fact that proceedings in the Congress were conducted in the highest manner of order and intelligence, probably were main factors in the newsmen's keeping their respect and refraining from name-calling Julia and the peace convention as a "visionary's tea party."

Another fascinating aspect of the women's movement is the only-human one of how they got along. Hardly less than the Ford Expedition, the Hague Congress was warm with avid newsmen all too eager to incite trouble for the sake of a head-line. It was clear that they were itching to report a cat-fight; with luck, a real hair-pulling match. They waited in vain, as Emily Balch recorded in her diary. "The women parted better friends than when they began," she assures us. These women, however, were not average. They belonged to a common tradition of learning of the highest caliber. H. G. Wells, a booster of the female pacifists, commented with incredulous "delight" upon the "Wellesley" of Emily Balch's time.

Nevertheless, a piece of pure "catting" on the part of the high-minded Emily is to be found in her graphic observations of her British counterpart, Mrs. Pethwick-Lawrence. The Eng-lishwoman enjoyed something of a "best-dressed list" reputa-tion.

This is Emily's description of the lady's costume:

> This evening Mrs. Pethwick-Lawrence spoke, a friendly rather blousy lady in an ultra gown of the following mate-rials swathed about her—brilliant green silk with large rose pattern in two shades of orange; black fur around part of neck and hanging in a tail behind her shoulders, crimson silk tight about the lower part, with a black and silver Egyptian scarf (adorned at the ends with large buttons with some sort of a rosette behind them) fastened very tight, across the breast diagonally, a lot of tarnished gold lace with crimson silk under it.

No doubt Emily was observing accurately every item of Mrs. Pethwick-Lawrence's personal toilet and dress, including the gauche tightness, but we have a feeling she enjoyed exposing the victim.

The envoys to the war capitals were Jane Addams, Dr. Aletta Jacobs, and Rosa Genoni of Italy. It was said that not since the Quakeress Mary Fisher set out to preach Christianity to the Grand Turk had there been such a medieval romance. Emily Balch, at first dubious of the very spectacularity of these pilgrimages, was converted by their success, at least insofar as serious reception was concerned. What impressed the women was the unanimity of feeling among the belligerents. Each side was fighting because the other was. This profound philosophical stalemate appears to have delighted the lady envoys. Everybody, including the combatants, was in abstract agreement.

One bit of bad timing was the arrival of the envoys in London directly after the sinking of the Lusitania. However, Sir Edward Grey sent Miss Addams cordial regrets that he could not see her because his oculist had forbidden him to use his eyes (this in a handwritten note). Security precautions prevented publication of many interchanges. Espionage possibilities in the project seem to have tantalized certain of the statesmen. The women themselves seem to have revelled in the "real palace" of Count Tisza of Hungary with its "many antechambers and lackeys." The Pope was amenable, but felt that leadership should come from the President of the United States. The official Italian reaction was that it was too soon to talk about peace now, but "maybe some day." Only France was positively anti-negotiation, "even the best," although Prime Minister Viviani declared—in deference to the women—he had drunk pacifism in his "mother's milk." In Paris the pacific ladies were closely tailed by gendarmes. Belgium's d'Avignon, a pragmatist, said he would rather the enemy left Belgium as a result of negotiations than have the armies fight over it twice.

Emily Balch, Christal Macmillan, and Rosika Schwimmer were among the Northern delegation. Even in those days, it apparently had become popular to pass the onus onto the United States. Mme. Schwimmer reported of the German ambassador

to Copenhagen that he was "very international-minded—
thought President Wilson had behaved very badly." King
Haakon VII kept the delegation so long that the women feared
they had missed some occult signal ending a royal audience. St.
Petersburg pleased the women because it was "clean and orderly."

Then they assailed the final bastion, the United States,
armed with the evidence. Wilson, as he was later to be to Ford,
was diplomatic. The hostile Colonel House wrote of the
women delegates in his diary: "As usual I got them into a controversy among themselves which delights me since it takes a
pressure off myself." He also reports with annoyance of the
Ford-Lochner interview that Lochner kept getting the conversation off interesting subjects and on to peace.

Now, as Jane Addams wrote, "an unexpected development
gave the conference of the neutrals adverse publicity and produced a great hilarity on two continents." The Ford Peace
Ship, into which Rosika Schwimmer had steered Henry Ford,
was the "unexpected development."

Neither Jane Addams nor Emily Balch ever went aboard
Oscar II, though both guiding light pacifists were billed as
being on. Emily's excuse is obscure, but Jane's plea of illness
was very real. She was hemorrhaging from the kidneys and was
slated for surgery. She had planned to sail with the Ford Peace
party despite her misgivings, which she explained this way:
"The offer of a crusading journey to Europe with all expenses
paid could but attract many fanatical and impecunious reform-
ers. With many notable exceptions, a group of very eccentric
people had attached themselves to the enterprise, so that there
was every chance of a fiasco." She points out that the Neutral
Conference became completely lost in the emphasis on the
Peace Ship. It was all form and no content. Notwithstanding
all this, she would have gone. She added: "I was fifty-five years
old in 1915; I had already 'learned from life' that moral results
are often obtained through the most unexpected agencies."

So it was that, a year after Rosika's personal visit with President Wilson urging him to call a Neutral Conference for Continuous Mediation, the chief executive remained unwilling to activate such a Conference. In the eyes of Mme. Schwimmer, Henry Ford became the perfect substitute for Wilson. She was aware of Ford's public declarations pledging to *do* something for peace. "Men sitting around a table, not men dying in trenches, finally settle the differences," was typical of Ford's peace remarks, and was good enough for Rosika's own creed.

Rosika had succeeded in obtaining a private visit with Henry Ford just a few days before she was to sail back for Europe. "If President Wilson won't call a Neutral Conference, why can't you, Mr. Ford? You're the man to do it," Rosika prodded hotly at his ego.

Henry Ford was beginning to feel the status and power of the "Leader of the Land," and he was galvanized with inspiration. "When I go into a thing, I jump in with both feet!" he declared after agreeing to launch the second Peace Ship, in behalf of American participation in a Neutral Conference.

Mr. Ford not only jumped in, but got both feet very wet. Aboard the Oscar II, he nearly drowned in an accident to which I can personally attest.

6

Stowaways, Newlyweds,
and Freeloaders

The reluctant host was one of the last to make the sailing party on December 4. Advisedly or not, he missed, or was spared, a great deal.

William Jennings Bryan, well-schooled for this sort of fête by his Chatauqua background, preceded, in a genial mood, the peace crusader he had come to see off at the Hoboken pier. Just the same, he was not alert enough to reject in time the presentation of a caged gray squirrel. By then he was stuck with the squirrel, and kept the cage under one arm for the rest of the festivities. It developed that a number of minds had conceived the same "nutty" symbol, and the number of squirrels (both gray and red) to be brought to the ship, where many ran up the rigging, amounted to infestation.

Entrepreneur Lloyd Bingham made the most of his chance to emcee the event. He balanced on the rail while presenting the delegates to the roaring or hooting mob on the pier. The clergy were especially fluent at this opportunity to address a well-mixed audience. The Rev. Jenkin Lloyd Jones, the patriarchal ecumenist of his day, with an interdenominational church in Chicago, a religious weekly, *Unity,* the Congress of Religion and the Browning student movement in his cure, offered an invocation, but his Santa Claus-like beard infected the crowd with a disrespectful mirth which effectually drowned out the prayer.

At 1:15 on that cold December day, the Ford family, accompanied by the sculptor, C. S. Pietro, drove up in a flivver. Regally, if not nautically clad, down to the sable lapels, Ford touched off a crowning sensation in the crowd. He appeared disconcerted, particularly by the prompt gift of a gray squirrel, but sustained a manful smile as he made his way on board.

On board ship he was just in time for the Sacrament of Holy Matrimony. Berton Braley, the bard of the voyage, was to become a benedict under circumstances right out of one of his own ballads.

Braley, known as the "hobo poet," was a correspondent for *Collier's.* Somewhat incongruously, he was to find his poetic metier not in peace, but in war. His collections are titled "Buddy Ballads—Songs of the A.E.F." and "In Camp and Trench—Songs of the Fighting Forces." However, Braley was not to be the only one to jump on the bandwagon when the U.S. entered the war.

The naiveté of the whole period—pre-war and wartime—is folksily reproduced by the popular rhymester. With phonetic spelling, dropped g's and a hayseed hero, Berton Braley ground out his homespun American what-the-hell sort of valentines:

> In the crackle of the rifles and the rumble of the guns
> There's an underlying rhythm which interminably runs
> To a mighty sort of ragtime, as the bullets whine and spat
> And machine guns split the eardrums with a vicious rat-a-tat.

In his "Thanksgiving—Somewhere in France," he soars to hard-boiled heroic heights, in the same genre of "An' my heart it jumps in a bust of glee" and "Give thanks that you ain't no slacker pup," with:

> But now, though I'm in the midst of death
> An' half of the time in hell,
> I taste adventure with every breath
> In the roar of the shot an' shell
> An' the rats may scamper an' cooties bite
> A habit that I abhor,
> But I'm in the thick of a man's sized fight
> An' it's one I'm thankful for!

In his wildest flights of patriotism, however, Berton Braley apparently did not forget his host of the Peace Expedition. In a sort of free plug for Ford, he commemorated his brief contact with him in an ode to "The Enchanted Flivver—Fairy Tale:"

> I went to deliver a flivver
> To Dan, that most wonderful boy
> It made me all over aquiver
> It filled me with laughter and joy.
> I flew over brooklet and river
> To give you this gift from the giver,

and so forth, with strenuous exercise of *flivver, shiver,* and *sliver.*

Always ready to use one rhyme to do the work of as many as possible, the light-hearted laureate of the Expedition had decided to combine the peace pilgrimage with a honeymoon, but in the melee attending the sailing, had not gotten around to making his fiancée, Marian Rubicam, his bride. Whether fearful of unfortunate publicity, or simply in the interests of publicity, fortunate or otherwise, the delegates voted to combine the sailing party with a wedding. With more clergy immediately available than ever officiated at any royal marriage, the liberal-minded Rev. Jenkin Lloyd Jones, noted for his success among the orthodox and heterodox, took a prayer book from under his beard. The solemnization of the rites before the ship

Rev. Jenkin Lloyd Jones, who performed the shipboard marriage of the Braleys, with Marian Rubicam (the bride).

set sail was accompanied by shrieks of the ship's whistle.

Jones concluded with the words, "By the authority vested in me by the states of New York and Illinois, I proclaim you man and wife." It was not until after his turn on the line which immediately formed to kiss the very pretty bride that a reporter pointed out that the marriage was invalid, since it had taken place in New Jersey. A howl went up from Bryan, who had not yet gotten to kiss the bride. The Captain settled this technicality by guaranteeing to repeat the ceremony, if ever they got out to sea.

Ford was bidden goodbye by a weeping Clara, and took up position at the rail, from which he tossed her roses. His comment, when asked what he thought of the "motley crew," was

Clara Ford, Henry and Edsel. WIDE WORLD PHOTOS.

Judge Ben Lindsey, the trial marriage advocate—at sea with Mrs. Lindsey. CULVER COLLECTION.

tactfully understated. "This crowd suits me exactly. It's just like a community. In a community we have old folks and young folks, rich and poor, men and women and children. Some persons are more prominent and others less. Some have more ability and others less. Our ship is just like that. It's just as though I had scooped up an average American community and transferred it to a ship. That's why I like this crowd. It's representative."

As a matter of fact, the peace ship was something of an undisinguished in the choppy gray waves, as he swam furiously to Ford, was going to sail instead of walk.

Lloyd Bingham gave a vigorous demonstration, varsity style, of how to beat war. Andrew J. Bethea, the Lieutenant Governor of North Carolina, proclaimed that Southern womanhood would forever be maintained on its pedestal. Governor Hanna of North Dakota apologized along with Judge Ben Lindsey (the juvenile-delinquency and free-love justice), for being there. Governor Hanna's excuse was that he had relatives in Sweden whom he ought to visit, and Lindsey, apparently unreconciled, moaned, "Oh, God, why am I here?"

As a brawl broke out over undisclosed issues on the pier below, the Oscar II began to vibrate with the actual process of getting under way. Hawsers were cast off and the gangway was pulled in, almost out from under those apparently still not certain whether they belonged to the all-aboard or the all-ashore. A climactic roar burst from the crowd, and cheers, hoots, shouts, music, whistles followed the Peace Ship as it moved slowly into the Hudson. Within the general tumult on dock, a particularly violent outbreak occurred. Someone was fighting his way through the crowd to the edge of the pier from which the Oscar's gangway had been withdrawn.

Amidst the screams of the bystanders, a splash went up as a man plunged into the icy waters, and his flailing arms could be distinguished in the choppy gray waves, as he swam furiously after the now fast receding ship. More whistles blew, and a

Tugs nudge Henry Ford's Peace Ship out of the harbor.

river tug changed course and nosed toward the December swimmer. He was hauled aboard, treated for shock, and sent to the hospital for observation, identifying himself, although his actual name was Urban Ledoux, as Mr. Zero, "swimming to reach public opinion."

Henry Ford, unaware of this final gesture, was last seen with only his good side—or the benign half of his face apparent, for he was described as looking "beatific." In this brief apotheosis,

Henry Ford was transfigured, patron saint of the Age of Innocence.

No sooner were they all at sea together than a moral problem arose. Like everything previously associated with the Peace Ship, this controversy was serious, grotesque, hilarious, especially as shades of ocean night closed around these pilgrims who yet were no puritans. Were Berton Braley and Marian Rubicam legally married?

Here was a heady dilemma for these arbiters of world strife to bite on. Clergymen, educators, settlement workers, journalists and other well-connected professions were represented abundantly on board, but there was no lawyer on the ship to interpret the matrimonial status of its lovers. The Captain's promise to make it legal according to the law of the high seas apparently had been only a device to get the ship out of the harbor. The only recourse was a referendum. A poll was taken of all the delegates, and for the first and only time in the Expedition, the vote was unanimous. It was a landslide in favor of legalized sex.

The carnival atmosphere of the sailing did not abate as the Peace Ship's newlyweds were jovially ensconced in the bridal cabin by their fellow pilgrims, who were to share this public honeymoon. The nuptial promise of the whole crate of doves released at the pier had been fulfilled, and if that symbolic bursting of the image of the Holy Spirit made Dean Marquis' Episcopal blood run cold, this is not recorded.

Nor was a dower wanting. A collection was spontaneously taken up, and a handsome wedding gift of U.S. 5, 10 and 20 dollar gold pieces was presented to the couple. Gold coins some of us would like to remember were still in public circulation. This practical present, however, didn't even last the voyage. There was a roulette wheel aboard (owned by Braley himself), and the gift was dissipated before the happy couple ever got to Europe, much less home.

Still, any newlyweds might have done much worse than have

Henry Ford waving farewell to the New York skyline. FORD ARCHIVES.

made their wedding trip on the Oscar II. Ford, ever the teetotaler, had to warn one member of his own staff, "You cut out the booze or I'll have you fired when you get back to the U.S." But the other passengers were not under any such threat. Entertainment and cuisine left little to be desired. A *Musik-Program* of the voyage lists among the orchestra's numbers *America Ouverture, Ett Bondbrollop, Alexander's Ragtime Band,* and the *Champagne Galop.* An *Afskeds-Middag* menu offers:

Potage a la Newa
Kogt Lax med sauce Hollandaise
Oksefilet a l'Anglaise
Skinke med Gemyse
Stegt Kalkun m. br. Kartofler
Kompot
Blommer
Kransekage
Frugt   Dessert   Kaffe

Thus from the standpoint of creature comforts, at least, the cartoons in the press of the day did the ship less than justice. One depicts the Oscar as a sinking tugboat with a placard on the bow asking, "Have you seen our 1916 model." Another featured a three-men-in-a-tub type vessel, with the "men" ample females in poke bonnets, singing, "We don't know where we're going, but we're on the way." John O'Keefe's ode to "The Flivvership" went

I saw a little fordship
Go chugging out to sea,
     And for a flag
     It bore a tag
     Marked 70 h.p.
And all the folk aboardship
Cried "Hail to Hennery!"

"The folk aboardship," Ford's "representative crowd," were

"We don't know where we're going, but we're on the way"

indeed variegated. A Who's Who of the Peace Expedition was compiled and distributed to all the European newspapers upon the party's arrival, but it is considerably misleading, since some of its most distinguished names, such as that of Jane Addams and William Jennings Bryan, for one reason or another, missed the boat. However, the contingent that did make it certainly qualified as a "motley crew."

The most serious of the forty delegates held themselves aloof from the "life" of the ship, and with Rosika Schwimmer, the "expert advisor," whose "little black bag" continued to be a quizzical trademark, spent most of their time closeted in staterooms working over their plans. One cynical interpretation of the retiring conduct of these highminded ones was that they had been the most acutely felled by *mal de mer*.

And of the more convivial delegates, such as S. S. McClure, noted for his articulateness on all subjects at all times; Governor Hanna, who behaved as if he were stumping the campaign trail; and the Rev. Messers Aked and Jones, of whom the camera men faked a picture playing leapfrog on deck; it might have been not simply that they were more frivolous, but that they had better stomachs.

There were some aged passengers, four children; there were the clergy, politicians, educators and businessmen; there were the students, among whom it seemed every co-ed was strikingly pretty; and thirty-four journalists and three newsreel movie men. One of the correspondents called the ship a "floating Chatauqua." Like any other "community," it quickly aligned itself into groups. The delegates' groups had a speaker every afternoon and evening, with question and discussion periods resembling for all the world a modern Peace Corps group. "The Ford Student Body" studied world problems and heard an address every morning from one of the delegates. The educators held a series of their own, culminating in their "Address to the Teachers of the World," wirelessed at Ford's expense on December 16. From their floating island, the delegates could bombard the world with their "longest gun in the world—the Marconi."

The Ship had its official song, "Peace and Prosperity," declaring, in somewhat sanguinary imagery:

> The submarine and battleship
> Have served the devil long and well

The bloody sword and Zeppelin
Will find their resting place in hell.

There was also an unofficial song, of more upbeat key, in the form of a parody on *Tipperary:*

Our Peace Ship party started with a sendoff at the pier
We don't know where we're going, but we're mighty glad we're here.
It's a seasick sort of voyage, over miles of ocean spray,
But we put our trust in Henry and with heart and head we say:
It's a long way to Copenhagen,
It's a long way to sail,
It's a long way to Copenhagen,
But we'll get there never fail.
Goodbye dear old Broadway,
Goodbye Herald Square,
It's a long long way to Copenhagen,
But peace waits right there.

Besides these lyric expressions, the Ship had its official news organ, *The Argosy.* It solicited contributions of not more than 200 words, in the form of news items, poems, tabloid fiction, and "humorous paragraphs." Some of these contributions are notable for their complete candor:

> . . . Some of us doubtless entered upon this Expedition tainted with a spirit of jest, looking upon it as a foolish if not foolhardy exploit of an ultra-rich idealist. With the passing of each hour of time, each league of sea, that feeling has diminished . . .

A wide-eyed student's-eye view of ship-life is preserved. He notes at once that discussion at all costs, as a way of life, seemed to be the primary rule. "We are to assemble twice each day for discussions, what we are to discuss being, it seems, a matter of secondary importance."

As for social relations, aboard ship, he has this to observe. "Everyone seems to be in awe of everyone else. We, especially,

THE REV. DR. CHARLES F. AKED
Playing Leap Frog Over the Rev. Jenkin
Lloyd Jones Aboard the Ford Peace Ship,
Oscar II, on Her Way to
Christiania, Norway.

the students, walk the decks on tiptoe and give everybody who passes a wide berth or a deferential bow. If two of us happen to be together and pass someone who has white hair or good clothes or shabby clothes or any feature whatever that our distraught imaginations think distinguishing, we nudge each other, in a whisper asking, 'Who is it?'"

Apparently, the chief figure of mystery of the ship was Rosika Schwimmer. The student writes wistfully; "There is one name that I should like to connect with a face—Madame Rosika Schwimmer. She vies with Mr. Ford himself in the frequency with which her name is mentioned. Indeed she seems to be 'source material' for all statements concerning prime ministers, ambassadors, belligerent or not, or anybody with a European twist. I can visualize her only as a row of morocco-bound books entitled 'Information about Europe.' "

But there was even more to Rosika Schwimmer than that, as I wrote in this letter to my mother from Norway.

Dear Ma:

You must excuse the writing, but the way this ship is pitching, my paper is a moving target. (Only we don't talk about targets on this Peace Ship.) *Everybody* has seasickness except Frau Schwimmer. Mme. Schwimmer looks like the slender mother in a fairy tale, ready to turn up her dress sleeves and take a pan of gingerbread men out of the oven, but, believe me, she's not made of gingerbread herself, as some of our men on board are! It has been all peace-business as usual with her. Tell Pop I'm getting more of an education in the few days on this ship than if I'd finished at Columbia.

Who do you think came over the Marconi yesterday? Elihu Root, and we got to hear his interpretation of international law before you folks did at home in New York! Well, it sounded like fighting words to some of the pacifists, "all other nations having a right to protest against the breaking down of the law," and so on. But in the condition all of us are in, when people rush out of the cabin, you can't tell whether they're protesting, or whether they're seasick!

I've just found out who Rosika Schwimmer really is. This will impress the girls! Do you remember *Tisza Tales*, that they used to beg me to read to them when I was trying to study? The author is none other than this great feminist. Well, I actually got a chance to speak to her—

such are the little opportunities when practically everybody is sick in their bunks. I mentioned her fairy stories of Hungary, and she lit up—her eyes are warm as well as penetrating when she smiles. So I took courage, and told her of our old argument. Did Elizabeth do right to tell the cruel Ludwig she was carrying roses, when she was actually carrying bread to the poor, as he had forbidden her to do? Well, Frau Schwimmer smiled, and said, "But, you see, we were telling of a saint. To a saint, bread or roses, does it make so much difference?"

You know, I'm not sure Henry Ford knows the difference either, so maybe that makes him a saint, as some say. Of course, he's been called a few other things, too. But do you remember the night Pop gave me my confirmation of the Oscar invitation, and said to me, "Son, what is this, you've got a telegram here from a fellow named Ford?" I just said, "Well, I guess my car's ready." I'll never forget his face!

Oh, here's something else that will impress the girls! Who do you think my cabin-mate is? The husband of Amelia Bingham! I'm afraid that's what we all call him, but actually, I believe that's what he calls himself. Since he was her press agent, it's kind of a Pygmalion-story. I'm afraid he's not as impressed as I am at our being cabin-mates—he kind of expected the star's dressing room. But he's always full of hijinks—everybody loves to have Lloyd around. That's how he caught this cold he's got, putting on his own little show for the crowd at Hoboken. It was raining, you know, but we couldn't get him down off the ship's rail. That's Lloyd, always clowning. Now the cold's settled on his chest. Every time I turned over last night—I turn over when the ship does—I could hear him coughing. Now, don't go worrying about *me*.

Of course you read about the three-ring performance at the pier. Don't let it fool you. Some people laugh when they don't understand, they laugh when they're afraid. This war is spreading. It could become a *world* war. What does it mean, really, when Elihu Root says that whatever a na-

tion does in protest against the violation of international
law, it does not do as a stranger nor as an intermediary, but
in its own right? It means that sooner or later there'll be a
showdown. Can you see either side backing down? Well, as
things are, I'm for Ford, bread, roses, whatever he's trying
to bring to Europe. What else is there?

Don't worry about anything. This is the Biltmore Hotel
on a hull, only more so!

Your loving son

Definitely the spirit of money-no-object registered sympathetically with me, as well as with the youthful college ob-
server. He exults: "such extravagance gets into one's blood.
One wants to rush to the rail and empty one's pockets in the
sea and shout, 'What do we care for expense!' "

The newsmen, no less organized than the pacifists, founded
the "Ancient and Honorable Order of The Vacillating Sons of
St. Vitus," with headquarters at the ship's bar, and their own
pledged commitment on the mission was to drink it dry before
they reached Norway.

Apart from all these groups were Ford and his own en-
tourage. Dean Marquis seldom left his side. Gaston Plantiff,
the Ford New York agent, was along to serve as paymaster and
business manager of the Expedition. There were the usual secretaries and typists, and at the disposal of Marquis, an ex-
football player bodyguard.

But Ford, at least for the first several days of the voyage,
made himself perfectly accessible. Two hours a day, one in the
morning and one in the afternoon, were set aside for a general
news conference, but apart from this, he mingled freely, and
the correspondents had plenty of opportunities to observe and
take notes for their stories.

In one of these interviews early in the voyage, Ford remarked that he could put $150,000,000 in cash into the work
then and there if it proved necessary. "Money is only good for
doing something with it," he remarked. "I want to stop this

Gaston Plantiff of New York, who held the purse strings, with his boss.

war." It was this sort of statement that produced journalistic results like the *New York Tribune* headline:

GREAT WAR ENDS
CHRISTMAS DAY
FORD TO STOP IT

As we have seen, the Expedition got under way with a bang, and another and another, from the "world's longest gun." The idea of holding the world captive audience, bombarding it with wireless messages from this floating stronghold, this sort of pirate peace ship off to stage its pacific raids on all the embattled capitals of Europe, was exactly the kind of situation that enraptured Ford. The first messages to go out were an additional farewell to Clara and a last briefing to his secretary, Liebold, whom Ford had gotten out of the way by placing him on vacation. But the next message to issue from the Oscar II was to be the longest ever sent, and the first radio sermon. It was the Rev. Dr. Aked's Sunday sermon in the dining saloon, more than two thousand words long, and it cost over a thousand dollars to send. It was never printed.

The sermon was relayed via Cape Race, Newfoundland, in fifty-word installments. To anyone who commented on the expense, Ford's answer was, "I can make fifty million in a minute."

Ford was so carried away by the new toy, the wireless, while he was at sea, a mechanism by which he could broadcast his beliefs to the world, that the Rev. Aked's sermon set a precedent, and thereafter, the public relations man (known as press agent then) was instructed to Marconi part of the main speech delivered each night of the voyage.

On December 6, the third day out, Congress convened in Washington. The next day the Joint Session heard President Wilson's formal recommendation, an enormously long address, looking toward "preparedness." The President traced the rationale of U.S. neutrality and discussed the commitments of Pan-Americanism at length, and then came down to the point: ". . . we do believe in a body of citizens ready and sufficient to take care of themselves . . . if our citizens are ever to fight effectively upon a sudden summons, they must know how modern fighting is done . . . The military arm of their government . . . they may properly use . . . to make their independence secure,—and not their own independence merely but the rights of those with whom they have made common cause . . . It is with these ideals in mind that the plans of the Department of War for more adequate national defense were conceived . . ."

This Congress called upon the President to enact a program calling for ten battleships, six battle-cruisers, ten scout-cruisers, fifty destroyers, and assorted submarines and gun-boats—all of it calling for an enormous appropriation. On this same day Congress was the recipient of a telegram from Henry Ford, "Somewhere in the Atlantic," challenging them: "We the citizens of the United States, now sailing to Europe on the steamship Oscar II, with the serious purpose . . . to deliver the men from the trenches and the women from their suffering and agonies and restore the peace of the world upon an honorable and just basis which will stop the mad race of competitive armament, do hereby earnestly petition and entreat you to give the Peace Mission your support and encouragement . . ."

Having taken off the gloves with the President of the United States, Ford turned his attention to all the crowned and un-crowned heads of state in Europe.

Not even Ford was naive enough to suppose that the identical Marconigrams sent to kings, kaisers and presidents would in themselves change their hearts. His main objective in all this was to "get peace talk going." Copies to all the newspapers was the important part of his wireless assault.

The Ford message to the belligerent potentates was not actually written by him, but by his staff of writers; but it had received his careful study and full approbation. The letter began by urging that interest in fixing blame for the war be discarded; it disclaimed any intention to intrude upon national ideals, and noted that there was enough in common in all these ideals to form a basis for peace. Then came the cry for an immediate truce.

"Must more lives be crushed out, more wives and mothers bereaved, before we recognize that Europe is bleeding to death . . . ?" The plan of the Neutral Conference was outlined, and the wire concluded with an appeal:

> Let the armies stand still where they are . . . so that the soldiers may be delivered back from another bitter winter in the trenches and sent back to their labors and their firesides. As there is no other way to end the war except by mediation and discussion, why waste one more precious human life?

For the sake of humanity,

> Respectfully yours,
> Henry Ford
> and 165 representatives of the
> people of the United States of America

But it was not only earnest appeals like these that were keeping the Oscar's tiny transmitter hot. The newsmen were continually hassling with each other to beat the others with their messages, many of which had been concocted in the form appropriate to the police reporting to which the New York correspondents especially had been accustomed. The atmospheric conditions were bad to start with, and the congestion sometimes jammed the wireless for days, which started the rumor that the top brass of the Expedition was censoring the stories. Actually, the reverse was true. Ford absolutely refused to inhibit the wiring of any of the stories, regardless of their content.

It was Captain William Hempel, reading the messages sent out from his ship to check that its neutrality had not been violated, who let Ford in on the scurrilous content of many of the newsmen's accounts. Ford remained perfectly genial and unperturbed. "Let them send anything they please. I want the boys to feel perfectly at home while they are with me. They are my guests. I wouldn't for the world censor them."

The shrewd businessman who had made such capital out of the Ford-joke never understood that he lived in a world which, if not purer, was at least expected to perpetrate its charlatanries with more finesse. The atmosphere of rowdiness which had launched the Model T was scuttling the Peace Ship.

Not even were all the reporters "neutral." A London newspaperman, whose application to sail had been denied by Ford's lawyers, was discovered traveling steerage, this nether section of the ship having been excluded in the contract. Not only was his ruse applauded by Ford, it was rewarded with an exclusive interview, which none of the American correspondents had been granted, and which naturally did not dispose them any more kindly toward their patron. The London reporter's gratitude for the favor accorded him was manifest in the headline over his story: "Ford a Prisoner in his Cabin, Chained to Bed by Secretary."

However, the reporters' escapades did not redound to their own interests in the long run. Many of them were fired from their papers on their return to the States. And, to be expected, one newsman of greater integrity, who had forborne prostituting the truth like his confreres, was sacked for not having done so.

Just like any other "representative community," the Peace Ship had its factions and its internal controversies, and unlike most other communities, its affairs were avidly attended by the sensation-loving newsmen, who almost outnumbered the delegates. The strongest impression given of the Ark of Peace was one that prompted the laconic Sorensen to compare it to another fabled "representative-community" vessel—Noah's Ark.

Yet the only two-of-a-kind aboard, and they had no business being there, were a couple of stowaways: both young boys, one remaining anonymous to history, a Danish citizen who just

wanted to go home "for Christmas." He was promptly put to
work in the galley. The other was a 20-year-old New Yorker,
Jacob Greenberg, who had gained access to the Oscar II by in-
venting a Bon Voyage telegram for delivery to the always
sought-after Inez Mulholland, the Juno-esque suffragette leader
from Manhattan.

While his Danish fellow-freeloader was peeling potatoes,
"Jake" was at first put to scrubbing decks, until Henry Ford
heard from the wireless room that the *New York Times* correspondent, a young fellow named Elmer Davis, had sent a long
and colorful "human interest" story about an ADT messenger
(American District Telegraph, predecessor to Western Union),
who was making the voyage as his uninvited guest. Two hours
after passing Sandy Hook, Jake was appointed Ford's official
messenger boy, assigned to carry his first, middle and final
messages to the newsmen.

Back in New York Jake Greenberg and family struck the
celebrity jack-pot. Reporters and photographers descended on
the Greenberg tenement flat on East Third Street, where his
widowed mother lived with a younger sister. To a reporter she
described her boy as a high-school "genius," but a drop-out
who had to support the family. She was quoted by another
"sob-sister" reporter as exulting, "Jacob has always wanted to
be President of the Ford factory. He is a bright boy, and I don't
see why he shouldn't at least get to be able to own a Ford car
by making a good impression on Mr. Ford on his trip. I expect
my boy to be a great help to Mr. Ford in stopping this war."

Mrs. Greenberg's expectations, however, were to prove to be
purely maternal visions. The golden touch with which the
whole peace voyage was solidly plated was not to rub off on
her boy, who scarcely rose, by material standards, at least,
above the ADT messenger status by which he gained entree to
the world of peace and plenty. The postscript to Jake's Jack-
and-the-beanstalk escapade later carried him not to fame and
fortune, but on to the New York relief rolls. Still, ever celebrity-

struck, he served as a sort of lifelong supernumerary at Downey's, a theatrical café on Eighth Avenue, with the soliloquies of Lear or Othello on his lips. Thereafter, he was known around Broadway as "Jake Shakespear."

But as the Peace Ship's stowaway sank to deeper obscurity than that of the Oscar's washroom in which he spent the first two hours of the voyage, his old East Side schoolmate, Irving Caesar, who sailed legitimately, and friendship with whom he never betrayed on the trip, was later to recall his ill-starred old buddy as sweet-natured, well-meaning, and idealistic, but with an unnerving and rather symbolic idiosyncrasy—a trick of disappearing. Out on a walk or out for an evening on the town, Jake would vanish seemingly into thin air, to turn up as an extra or small bit-player in a New York film production, or as a stage "corpse" in a Broadway play.

Jake Greenberg played his last "death scene" in 1964, when he passed away in utter poverty and obscurity. One of the few genuine "legends" of the Peace Ship, he is remembered and anecdoted in many writings more often than are many of the Peace Ship's principal passengers.

7

"Freedom" of the Seas

"Mutiny on Board!" was the big Peace Ship headline to flash round the world on December 13. This was also the day the wireless cracked with angry messages from President Wilson in the White House, demanding that Austria punish the guilty U-boat commander who had sunk the liner Ancona, that reparations be paid over, and that compliance be prompt. A break in diplomatic relations was threatened.

Also that same day a headline from the Peace Ship might well have read, "Man Overboard!—Henry Ford swept into the North Atlantic!"

The ship had been nine days out before the early morning that its patron emerged from his cabin to the sea-swept upper deck of the violently listing and pitching small vessel. Done up more for the Easter Parade on Fifth Avenue than for a constitutional on deck in midwinter, Ford was austerely resplendent in his now familiar sable-collared coat and derby.

This writer, the youngest of the newsmen aboard the Peace Ship (whose birthday that morning went unnoticed and un-fêted), had also come on deck at that stormy early hour. A bad

94

Henry on deck in front of his stateroom where, later, his life was saved. CULVER COLLECTION.

sailor, since this was the first of some one hundred and ten subsequent trans-Atlantic crossings, I slumped into one of Ford's personal deck-chairs with that sinking, nauseous feeling in the stomach which characterizes that most disagreeable of illnesses —*mal de mer*. This was not the promenade deck, but the one above, immediately under the bridge, and it was reserved exclusively for Ford's daily walks. I chose this deck as a refuge away from the derisive stares of the good sailors on the promenade deck. There was the Head Man, pacing unsteadily in front of his cabin. Here at last was Henry Ford alone and I had him to myself. If I could only suppress the compulsion to puke and say "Good morning, sir, I represent—" But the vertiginous sway made me shut my eyes while my non-seasick subconscious reporter self told me I was missing my big chance.

Suddenly there was a pitch, then a quiver of the propellers, and the Oscar II seemed to soar out of the water as if poised for a take-off into space. As the ship nosed back onto the sea, I heard a thud and a clatter, and when I opened my eyes I saw Ford's gold-handled cane and derby (no one had told him canes and derbies were not for shipboard promenading) sliding across the deck, and with them Henry's slight frame. He was coasting fast through the inch-deep water of the listing deck straight for the opening between the life-boat davits and railing, wide enough, in those days before the Coast Guard regulation, for the body of a man to go through. Seasickness had not completely blunted my youthful reflexes, and I sprang from the chair and grabbed him by the first part that came handy—the sable collar—and got him back on his feet. Then I made for the derby and the cane and restored them to a flustered and slightly damp automobile tycoon who must have heard me say," Nasty weather, sir." To this incredible understatement he replied with his customary taciturnity, "Yep, sure is—" Then he thanked me for saving his hat and cane and quickly disappeared into his cabin!

I resumed the seasick role, closing my eyes to the heaving horizon and to the entire incident, which I never mentioned to my colleagues. Perhaps I felt that my host would be embarrassed. I certainly had no thoughts of advertising myself as a life-saver, especially when Ford himself seemed to look upon me as the rescuer of his bowler and gold-handled cane. Not until later—eighteen months later—when I received a personal invitation to visit and lunch with him at Dearborn was there anything but the most casual allusion to that incident on the upper deck of the Oscar II. I was always convinced that while we both dismissed it as an "incident," the unspoken assessment was of a near tragedy.

Here is how I wrote of it in a letter to my mother and her reply follows:

Dear Ma:

And who do you suppose is responsible that Henry Ford is alive today? That's right, your son. Don't expect to read about it in the papers. I'm too embarrassed to put it in my dispatches, and I'm sure he's too embarrassed. But I got a good grip on his sable collar (yes, it's sable, all right!) just in time to save him from the waves. He was coasting down the deck at a thirty-degree grade in six inches of water straight for the opening under the rail. He's thin, as you can tell from his pictures, and he could never have caught himself.—Maybe he'll give me a car! Then you *will* have something to worry about! Me, in a tin lizzie riding around Stuyvesant Park!

You know, it seems a funny thing to say about our host, but I'm a little sorry for Mr. Ford. On this ship of great brains and fire-eaters, he acts rather outside of things. I found out where he's been spending his time—down in the engine room. That's the kind of wheels and fire he understands. But the dousing he got has quarantined him even from the mechanical workings of this ship. The grippe and seasickness have laid down most of the pacifists. Poor Lloyd Bingham got it bad. They moved him to a larger state-room yesterday, so he's in solitary splendor, befitting the star's husband.

From all the reports we get on the Marconi we're a floating news agency. I'm not sure whether I'm approaching the thick of the fighting or have just gotten out of it. Some-

times it sounds like the biggest fight is between the "preparedness" and the "anti-preparedness" crowd, and I just
wonder how long this ship can stay out of that scrap!
Maybe Mr. Ford took to his bed just in time.

Now listen to this! (especially Pop). I met Henry
Bernstein—editor of The *Day*. Told him how I poured over
his "With Master Minds."

I've also found out a little more about the woman of
mystery, Mme. Schwimmer, and she's certainly a lady of
many traits. When she was a girl, they couldn't decide
whether she'd be a concert singer or a pianist, and she surprised them all by writing a cookbook and a child care
manual. Apparently she went through the arts and the
domesticity young, to turn her attention to international
things now. But the background accounts for her great
poise and personality and also the bib-and-apron coziness.
Yet when I see her in her hat with the black plumes and
that little black bag of hers, I think of those spooky *Tisza
Tales* of hers, and believe she's out of one of her own Hungarian legends.

Hello to everybody on East 17th Street, and love to the
girls.

Your loving son

Dear Son:

Why do you hide your light under a bushel? If I say my
son saved the life of Henry Ford, who believes me? You're
too modest. But I know you did it out of the goodness of
your heart, not like some people. Everybody's in the papers
these days and wants to get their two cents in, they're carried away. You always had a level head. Still, if he wants to
do the right thing by you, don't refuse him.

Now Wilson seems to be changing his tune. It's the
times. It's building up. They say nothing ever hit the civilians like the U-Boat sinkings and the Belgian stories. Belgium is the heroine, shown on posters like the Statue of
Liberty. It's the symbol. An atmosphere is building up.

What a time to pick for a Peace Ship! It's like fate.

How is poor Mr. Bingham, better? His wife should be with him. I feel for him, but not to the extent you should catch cold, too. Be careful, with all those sick people. And in Norway the weather will be bitter, don't get a chill. I will send you some cookies, hope they will get through.

What did Mr. Ford say to you when you saved him?—

Your father says to say he will write. Don't hold your breath. Lots of kisses from the girls. Without you it's not natural.

Love,

Ma

Ford's life had been saved, but not that of his mission, which gave off signs of foundering even before it reached Europe. The dousing had its effect on the wiry but rather frail tycoon. A heavy cold became complicated, and as if *mal de mer* had not already sufficiently depleted the Expedition, another gallicized malaise, *la grippe*, rendered its leader *hors de combat*.

Could Ford's continued functioning as a polarizing force have somehow salvaged what was already the wreckage of the Expedition? That remains one of many points for retrospective speculation, along with the disruptive effect of Mme. Schwimmer's secret weapon, the "little black bag," and her volatile personality which caused her to respond to welcoming applause with "Don't be hypocrites!"

In any case Ford's near-drowning, a complete secret to the world (except to my folks) on and off ship, was a vital link in a chain of ensuing misfortunes. As soon as Ford was felled, of course, he was at the mercy of two forces, separate yet combined in their destructive policy toward the Expedition—the gloomy Dean whose very presence was dedicated to the purpose of getting Ford back home, and the newshawks dedicated to getting a story, and preferably a scandal. And each one was grist for the other's mill.

One delegation of newsmen succeeded in intimidating Ford's

man into letting them into the sick-cabin, and challenged their bunk-ridden host thus: "Mr. Ford, J. Pierpont Morgan was dead six hours before any newspaper knew about it. We won't be scooped that way this time. So we've come to see for ourselves whether you are still alive."

Ford, a man who lived by "hunches," was no doubt uninspired by this visitation. Also, a partner of as close-knit a marriage as the Fords' is apt to become homesick during illness, and probably Ford was already thinking longingly that "it was time to get home to mother."

What really did happen when the Mutiny headlines crackled over the airwaves? What was the "war in mid-ocean?" Did S.S. McClure roar at the top of his lungs that he would never sign the anti-preparedness resolution? Did Lochner accuse him of coming on a colossal joy-ride? What was behind the reporters' stories of fist-fights and drawn pistols? Did the patriarchal Dr. Jones shake his fist at McClure and bellow, "Go to—bed!"?

I was within earshot of that explosion and I trembled in fear for the reverend's long, white beard, having found out early in my journalistic novitiate all about the "mad" McClure, the "Blond Beast" of *McClure's* Magazine, the splenetic and unpredictable S.S. of the McClure Syndicate ("father of American newspaper syndication"). Because there were, among the peace delegates who gathered in the main dining saloon that night, other accomplished artists of the abrasive and vituperative phrase, the clash of temperaments was inevitable. Over and above the shouts of those assembled who wanted McClure to "sit down," the bumptious S.S. jumped on a banquette and pulled from his coat pocket an advance copy of President Wilson's "preparedness speech," which he had received before sailing in his capacity as editor of the *New York Daily Mail*. McClure managed to read the message to the bewildered delegates at the precise moment it was being delivered to the Joint Session of Congress in Washington. Only a city desk boss with

"S.S." McClure—
infant terrible of
the Peace Ship.
N.Y. WORLD NEWS
SERVICE.

an inflexible fidelity to release dates would have been capable
of such timing.

This was the historic Third Annual Message, which consti-
tuted Wilson's departure from his strong "too proud to fight"
neutrality of only two months before, and was to pave the way
for his big Western preparedness tour. In his strident tones, Mc-
Clure read:

> At least so much by way of preparation for defense seems
> to me to be absolutely imperative now. We cannot do less.

The detailed program for a vastly strengthened navy, for a
citizen army and a merchant marine capable of the "revival of

our old independence," the greatly increased revenue to support it, concluded:

> What we are seeking now . . . is national efficiency and security . . . to make (the nation) sufficient to play its part with energy, safety, and assured success.

McClure wound up with a vigorous argument in support of the President's plea for preparedness.

The delegate from New York immediately countered this. "We are going abroad now on a mission to stop a terrible war among nations, every one of which is prepared in a military way for war." He closed with a resounding appeal for a protest against Wilson's recommendations.

Then there followed the "discussion" of which radio reports varied so widely, from "Healthy, Animated Airing of Views" to "War in Mid-Ocean" and "Uproar on the Peace Ship." At any rate, there was enough to alert a passing refugee from the "Ancient and Honorable Order of the Vacillating Sons of St. Vitus" (the name given by the newsmen to their inner circle of hardy imbibers), who without doubt had been living up to the prime commitment of his brotherhood in the bar, with the good news: "The big story's broken! They're having a fight!" "Mutiny on board!" There was a stampede toward the Marconi room.

The pacifists remained parliamentary, even in disorder, and elected a committee of five to draft the Peace Ship's anti-preparedness resolution—a rebuttal to Wilson's "militarist doctrine." However, partly to smooth the matter over, and partly in the assumption that all the delegates would be anti-preparedness, they announced that instead of holding open debate, the resolution would be left available for a period of five days for the delegates' scrutiny, then—signatures.

McClure immediately fired up. "For years I have been working for international disarmament . . . But I cannot impugn the course laid out by the President of the United States and

BY WIRELESS FROM THE PEACE-SHIP.
—Bartholomew in the Minneapolis *Daily News*.

supported by my newspaper. I should like to be able to go on working with the delegation, but I am unable to sign that part of its declaration of principles which would place me in opposition to my Government."

The delegates swiftly divided up into sides. Judge Lindsey, Governor Hanna, journalist John D. Barry, the Harvard-bred columnist for the *San Francisco Bulletin* and author of some dozen popular novels of his day, and others stood with McClure. Mme. Schwimmer and Jenkin Lloyd Jones opposed them, and McClure was accused of "corrupting" the student delegates and of having come for a free ride.

The correspondents leaped into the breach with a spontaneous mock trial in the main saloon, dragging in the nonplussed and ailing Henry Ford to preside, and upbraiding him for being a party to "steamroller tactics" and of trying to "railroad" the resolution through.

Ford's only comment on the proceedings was, "Do you remember how the President advised us to take only pacifists with us? Well, I guess we've followed his suggestion."

"Pacifist," observed young William Bullitt, reporter of the *Philadelphia Ledger*, "means a person hard to pacify." He found brutal confirmation of this when, nineteen years later, he was United States Ambassador in Moscow.

The breach was healed as well as might be by a statement prepared by the staff but signed by Ford, emphasizing acceptance of the resolution by all the delegates on the "Crusade," although proposing that to work for peace while condoning preparedness was illogical.

But from the point of view of the Expedition's "image" the amelioration was useless. The *Chicago Tribune* correspondent proclaimed, "The dove of peace has taken flight, chased off by the screaming eagle." A four-box cartoon strip depicted the Ford delegates first with their arms around each other singing "We're all for peace!" then, "What *kind* of peace?" and finally, in a wild free-for-all of fisticuffs, "Peace at any price!"

Mary Alden Hopkins, the Wellesley-bred neo-Malthusian research journalist, was to remark later, "The amount of wrangling has been picturesquely exaggerated." However, she added cryptically, "A man does not become a saint by stepping on a peace boat." Lochner had to defend the Expedition: "Show me any live community in which there is not healthy disagreement over details." But even he admitted later that "the closing days of our voyage were not a symphonic poem."

For a young man trained in circumspect discourse, this was a glaringly bold pronouncement.

The Peace Expedition neared land—the Orkney Islands, north of the Scottish coast—to the tune of jokes in Parliament over Henry Ford. Lord Rosebery spoke in Edinburgh of "a vessel coming over at this moment fraught with peace and propelled by a gentleman named Ford, said to be a manufacturer of perambulators." These welcoming notes were relayed to the delegates by wireless, heightening the tension aboard as to what the British Navy would do about Oscar II.

On December 15, the routine shot was fired across the bow of the Peace Ship. By a succession of fine ironies, the Oscar was anchored directly opposite Lord Rosebery's imposing castle, and the boat bringing the British boarding party was the Pax Vobiscum, and that bearing the harbormaster was The Good Shepherd.

The officer, a middle-aged lieutenant of the Royal Navy, led the boarding party over the side from the rope ladder, and his first words to the Captain as he touched the deck were, "You didn't really mean you had a mutiny on board, sir, did you?"

The Captain shook his head and smiled reassuringly.

"That's what the navy thought," was the lieutenant's rejoinder.

Later the harbormaster assured the leaders of the Ford party that they had debated coming to the rescue, having figured out that the wireless messages were just "American newspaper talk." When the entire contingent of navy men, all of them marines and most of them wearing heavy beards, was on board, a thorough search of the Ship began. It was the same sort of British thoroughness which was exercised in the decision to hold up the Oscar II from early Wednesday morning until Thursday night. The vessel waited outside the harbor for more than sixteen hours, because no ship was permitted to enter in the hours of darkness. The fareway was closed until daylight by spar booms and floating mines which guarded the passage.

The ship was detained for two days for the surprising reason that contraband was found in the hold—albeit contraband worthy of a vessel bearing many vegetarians: dried fruit! However, the British ruled that the Oscar might proceed to Christiania (Olso), on condition that the dried fruit be left at Kirkwall.

The detention of the Oscar was a striking instance of the efficiency of the British blockade. The wireless was "sealed." Hence there was no communication with the neutrals nor anyone else. All cables were closely censored ashore before mailing to London for transmission to the newspaper addressees in the States. Letters had to be sent ashore unsealed.

The mass of mail from the Peace Ship swamped the censor. Harbormaster Downes put on two extra men—war workers above military age—and they put in an entire night reading the newspaper copy alone. Many correspondents had ignored the regulation against sealing their dispatches, and these had to be opened and resealed.

One irony in which the delegates found little humor was that the thousands of Christmas-gift-wrapped presents which had been chosen to bring pleasure to the children of Scandinavia, were all torn open and searched—for ammunition! On a Peace Ship, if you please!

The Oscar had been on the high seas just under two weeks before reaching Kirkwall, and this detention, within tantalizing sight of land, was in itself chafing to the delegates, many of whom had long since been getting on each other's nerves. And the creature-comforts of warmth and baths being lacking, while lying in harbor, added to the general edginess. Nevertheless, the delegates from the Middle West were particularly excited by this "capture" by the British warships. Two middle-aged ladies asked the British sailors if they might feel their guns. Ford was greatly charmed by three Scots, whom he requested to have brought to his cabin. The harbormaster was

"THE TUG OF PEACE"

Above is the reproduction of a cartoon in "Punch" of London. The drawing has reference to the peace mission led by Henry Ford, and reflects the English viewpoint from which Mr. Ford's expedition is regarded.

cordial, but to his good wishes were added his own condition for peace, Germany's decisive defeat.

Some delegates attempted to jump ship, but the only one who made it was the British reporter, proclaiming that he had scooped them all.

By one account, Mme. Schwimmer's last-ditch attempts to rally the delegates to a spirit of unity for the benefit of a forthcoming meeting with the press were to backfire. Mme. Schwimmer and her "little black bag" had sufficiently alienated enough people so that her disclosure that the "unseen documents in the bag had nothing whatsoever to do with the Expedition," did not mend the rift.

In any case, McClure disavowed his own fidelity to the "statements" read to the Norwegian press, in such vitriolic terms and in so menacing a stance, that the statuesque Inez Mulholland (Boissevain) had to leap between him and loyal Lochner, imploring them not to "resort to a militaristic settlement." Miss Mulholland, the reigning beauty of the ship, was more successful than Frau Schwimmer.

The rank-and-file of the passenger list had mostly recovered from seasickness, but many were bedded down again with the flu that had spread over the ship like an epidemic. One of the mascots, a squirrel from Hoboken, curled up and died at sea. Which rodent it was, the one named "Henry Ford," or the one named "William Jennings Bryan," was never established.

This last lap of the voyage had been fraught with peril that made a harbor—any harbor—welcome under any circumstances. The North Sea was the old field of the lurking submarines. Eight months before, a ship was blown up there daily. As the Peace Ship ploughed on, with the snow-capped mountains of Norway lying along her port rail, the lifeboats hung from the davits ready for action, side lights were burning and the Danish flag at the helm stood out in bold illumination, so that no chance marauder should mistake the identity of the Peace Ship.

The next few hours were probably the most dramatic of the entire voyage. Few had gone to bed and most of the peace party were up, fully dressed, sitting in the lounges and lining the deck rail—waiting. No one would admit that fear had entered the minds and thoughts of the peace advocates and was temporarily—as in a double-print on film—super-imposing itself on their visions of truces, peace conferences, doves! Instead there were recent newspaper headlines of U-boat sinkings, photos of panic-stricken, shrieking passengers rushing for lifeboats along listing decks. . . . *Spoorlos versenkt!*

While the clergy offered prayers, the politicos argued pro and con the nature of the enemy, the reasons for the war and the most disturbing of all subjects—U.S. preparedness. It was hardly a debate. The talk, lasting into the early morning hours, was clearly an accumulation of words which did not have the chance to be said while the ship was in mid-ocean. In Germany's back-yard, with the power of Admiral von Tirpitz's submarines presumed ready and able to send all to the bottom, the less rabid of the pacifists and a few of the reluctant guests who had come along for the ride, began firing a few torpedoes of their own.

It was one thing to fall asleep in your comfortable bed at night after eloquent encomiums upon the country because it hesitated to retaliate on the Germans for killing helpless civilians. It was a piece of the same illogic—and indeed very Christian—to turn other people's cheeks while damning the torpedoes, but not the barbarians who fired them. It was quite something else again to find yourself far from the safety of your pulpit confronted by the prospect of a hostile periscope and a Teuton U-boat commander who held the power of life and death over you. Retaliation being the foundation of warfare, it was on many a pacifist mind that night.

"*Schreklichkeit*"—frightfulness—horror: horror pure, naked, hellish, was the other side of the golden coin of the pacifist vision. *Schreklichkeit,* the negative of the vision—the black side, the catalogue of German atrocities, broke with fracturing violence upon the eyes of the world, particularly of the New World, whose sons and daughters were suddenly here in U-boat infested waters.

Never before had war hit civilians like this. It was the German violation of freedom of the seas and of neutrality, of the rights of neutrals, that evoked such furious reaction from the outpourings of writers, editorialists and statesmen like Wilson and Lansing. Their notes on the sinking of the Lusitania, and the subsequent sinking of the Gulflight, the Cushing, the Arabic and literally thousands of tons of ships listed in Jane's World Directory of Shipping, flashed before all like a nightmarish newsreel. When the Oscar II sailed cautiously into these northern waters, it actually ploughed across a huge cemetery—of ships.

Of the torpedoing of the Lusitania, which cost 1,198 lives, of which 128 were American, the Oscarites endorsed Bryan's note to the full and expressed with him "concern, distress, and amazement." Bryan, "one of us," warned that "the imperial German Government will not expect the Government of the United States to omit any word or any act necessary to the performance of its sacred duty of maintaining the rights of the United States and its citizens and of safeguarding their free exercise and enjoyment."

This doctrine was strong stuff coming from Pacifist Bryan, but it was also expounded by Elihu Root, a former Secretary of State and a recipient of the Nobel Peace Prize in 1912, in an address delivered by him at the annual meeting of the American Society of International Law in December, 1915, while the Peace Ship was at sea. Excerpts came by wireless.

"International laws violated with impunity," said Root, "soon cease to exist, and every state has a direct interest in preventing those violations which, if permitted to continue, would destroy the law. Wherever in the world, the laws which should protect the independence of nations, the inviolability of their territory, the lives and property of their citizens, are violated, all other nations have a right to protest against the breaking down of the law. Such a protest would not be an interference in the quarrels of others. It would be an assertion of the protesting nations' own right against the injury done to it by the destruction of the law upon which it relies for its peace and security. What would follow such a protest must in each case depend upon the protesting nation's own judgment as to policy, upon the feeling of its people and the wisdom of its governing body. Whatever it does, if it does anything, will be done not as a stranger to a dispute or as an intermediary in the affairs of others, but in its own right for the protection of its own interest." Good old standard American doctrine!

A note from Secretary of State Lansing declared that "the sinking of passenger ships involved principles of humanity which throw into the background any special circumstances," and that "the principal fact is that a great steamer, primarily and chiefly a conveyance for passengers, and carrying more than a thousand souls who had no part or lot in the conduct of the war, was torpedoed and sunk without so much as a challenge or a warning, and that men, women, and children were sent to their death in circumstances unparalleled in modern warfare."

And of the sinking of the Ancona by an Austrian submarine, Lansing wrote "the conduct of the commander can only be characterized as wanton slaughter of defenseless noncombatants . . ." that "the United States . . . demand that the Imperial and Royal Government denounce the sinking of the Ancona as an illegal and indefensible act . . . and it rests this expectation on the belief that the Austro-Hungarian Government will not sanction nor defend an act which is condemned by the world as inhumane and barbarous, which is abhorrent to all civilized nations . . ."

On this last night, some passengers went to the upper decks to be near the lifeboats, some slept in their steamer chairs. Oddly, it was the first tranquil night of the entire voyage on the water; the passengers needed tranquilizers. A full moon touched the waves with silver. Out of the great combers of the Atlantic, the violent pitching and listing that had relegated so many delegates to sick bay in the early days of the voyage now subsided.

The British had done an extraordinary job of sweeping the vast expanse of the North Sea clear of hostile craft and floating mines. The Ark of Peace passed unmolested to her port.

And the undaunted delegates were heartened by still another delusion, that of a royal welcome in Norway promised them by Rosika Schwimmer. The Expedition sailed into port at a renewed pitch of fervor. Henry Ford had said, "Every nation in the world will soon look upon the American peace pilgrimage as taking the initiative in stopping history's worst war.

The landing of the Peace Expedition in Europe will be recorded as one of the most benevolent things the American Republic ever did."

Mary Alden Hopkins lent her lyric voice to the idyllic vision, although the physical circumstances—hour, 4 a.m. of a Sunday, and temperature, twelve below zero—could hardly conduce to a tumultuous welcome:

"One hundred and fifty everyday people have been brought face to face with a great idea—the thought of world disarmament," wrote Miss Hopkins. "There's no escaping it, short of jumping into the sea. The idea pervades the ship. Groups talk of it . . . Reporters are nervous lest there's no news value in it . . . At times the vision comes to all of us—mystic, veiled, and wonderful. The common sense revolts. Yet we dare not treat the vision with contempt. A ship of fools crossed the Atlantic in 1492. A ship of fools reached Plymouth in 1620. Can it be that in this ship of common fools, we bear the Holy Grail to the helping of a wounded world?"

Henry Ford, imbued with like fervor, if with little lyric voice, made a prophecy of his own, in more pedestrian terms:

"Wait until I land and watch developments."

8

The Christiania Turn

Unfortunately, the enveloping winter haze which pervaded the Norwegian midwinter air seemed also to effect a clouded crystal ball.

In the bemusing atmosphere of a Christmas card, from the landlocked harbor of Christiansand where the rocky coastal hills thrust into the water, the Oscar II slipped along a snow-covered shore of pine-spiked hills under an inky sky frosted brilliantly with stars.

The feelings of the peace pilgrims at the sight of land were focused for us in "Memento," written on the occasion, for the pacifists were never quite too moved for words.

Irving Caesar, the young stenographer from New York's Lower East Side, who was never at a loss for words, and who was later to soar to great heights on Tin Pan Alley, authored this:

MEMENTO

CHRISTOPHER COLUMBUS, greetings! This moment we truly live with you. We too have crossed the ocean. And ours too was a mission—a real mission.

You went because you knew, you had faith, you believed.
This was a round world, and there, far, far, you knew India
was. You were right. It was.

You set sail and you sailed, weeks and weeks and months
and months. The voyage was tempestuous, but you minded
not, for you knew, you had faith, undying faith.

Then you saw land, real land, where there were humans,
and animals and birds and flowers.

No, it was not India. But that matters not. It was a greater,
grander India—a new World.

We too have faith. We too have gone—not to discover, but
to rediscover God's world.

We may not find our India, we may not stop this war, but
we will find a greater India. We will plant the little acorn
that shall grow the oak under whose shade shall thrive, not
peace in Europe, or America, Asia or Africa, but peace on
earth, in every man, in every woman, in every child.

Columbus, greetings! We now sight land, even as you once
did. You had faith and you were repaid. We too have faith!
Will God forget?

December 14, 1915   Off Shetland Island
                                               Coast of Scotland

Within the next few years Irving will have earned over a million dollars by writing the lyric of that perennial hit song, "Tea
for Two" and collaborating with Vincent Youmans on the
Broadway musical *No, No Nanette*. He also became the first
collaborator of George Gershwin, with whom he wrote
"Swanee," "I was So Young and You Were So Beautiful," and a
thousand other song verses which have kept him to this day in
a top ASCAP (American Society of Composers and Publishers)
royalty bracket.

Like a ghost the big ship slid smoothly into the Christiania
(now Oslo) pier at 5 a.m., fully five hours before a typical Norwegian day would get under way, for here in midwinter it did

not really even start to get light until nine o'clock, and people seldom got to work before ten.

Mme. Schwimmer had forecast a resounding welcome. The pier was deserted. After the tardy Norwegian dawn at about 9 a.m., a party of about twelve Norwegians appeared to greet the ship. When the delegates eagerly disembarked, they were met with no more interest than some local group coming back from a day's fishing excursion.

Throughout the crossing, Mme. Schwimmer, operating in the "dreamworld" in which she had said Ford's munificence had cast her, had assured the delegates of the gala welcome to be looked for in Norway.

Actually, the pacifists might have taken warning from the eight Norwegian and Swedish newspapermen who had boarded the Oscar II at Christiansand, to be promptly spirited to a second-class cabin-room by some of the more playful New York reporters for a comradely "briefing" on the voyage's goings-on.

The delegates had just concluded, they had hoped, an accommodation on the preparedness-unpreparedness controversy that had blown up to the "mid-ocean war," with the balance falling in favor of unpreparedness.

With this resolution to present, they were invading a country that had just voted an increase in the Army and Navy and strengthening of all defenses! The Norwegian reporters emphasized that to talk unpreparedness to this nation would be a disastrous mistake, and discouraged strongly any expectation on the part of the delegates of official recognition. Norway was walking the tightrope of strict neutrality. She was fearful of the slightest indication of tipping her precarious balance one way or the other.

Norway had firmly made the opposite commitment from that of the delegates. There was universal conscription. There was a standing army of 150,000 to a population of 3,000,000. Enor-

mous appropriations for defense had been voted over the preceding two years. Unlike the Peace Ship women, Norwegian women were militant. Preparedness was a national slogan.

But the delegates were too exhilarated by their destination in itself to be much crestfallen over the lack of fanfare accorded their arrival. It was a tingling, frost-silvered morning. Sleds jangling with bells were driven by men in Cossack hats and bearlike astrakhan coats. The delegates' luggage, all carefully tagged, in scrupulous Scandinavian contrast to the melee at Hoboken, was loaded on these sleds to be driven to the Grand Hotel. The delegates then took other sleds or taxis to the hotel, but not so their sponsor. Through the snow-banked streets, Henry Ford walked. It would be of interest to know whether Dean Marquis encouraged or tried to dissuade Ford from this feat of fool-hardihood, but here we have no record.

Henry Ford landed in every sense of the word. He was as glad as anyone to get his land-legs again, probably gladder than most. It was his first really convivial appearance among his pacifist confreres, and it was his last.

The peace party spontaneously planned a sightseeing excursion. Having already chartered a ship, chartering a train came easy. They took a train of cars up the electric railway running up the mountain out of the city. In the beautiful natural park, "Holmenkollen," then, as now, was a championship ski-run commanding a telescopic view of the city and the bay, which, with its medieval-fortress-like stone skyline somewhat resembled Quebec. The delegates borrowed some of the exuberant spirits of the ruddy, husky Norwegian boys and girls frolicking with snowshoes and skis.

The weather was crystalline. On this idyllic elevation in the rarified air, the delegates took a respite from pressing peace business to snowball each other and hike through the crunching, solid snow. But none outdid their patron. Henry Ford, still wearing the sable-collared coat, ploughed solo up the mountainside through drifts higher than he was. Not even northern Michigan had ever been like this. Who ever heard of a man in a derby and carrying a cane in a Michigan snow pile?

It was hard to tear themselves away from a view like a Christmas stereopticon with slope upon slope of glittering white, saw-toothed with the solid ranks of fir trees, the load of snow lowering their branches, and toylike figures of Norsemen and their women traveling on their skis or sleds with long, slender poles trailing as rudders behind.

But the first test of the Peace Delegation in Europe was impending. The initial meeting on foreign soil was scheduled to take place by invitation of the Norwegian section of the Women's International Peace League. That was to be in the late afternoon. But the real premiere would be in the evening, a public meeting at the University of Christiania.

This program gave the delegates just time to get back to the Grand Hotel, headquarters for the delegation, although some were accommodated at nearby hotels, none further than a couple of blocks away. Here, they tried to acclimate to the sumptuousness of their rooms and some necessary feats of computation.

A kroner was worth 27¢ in American money: a half kroner 13¢ and a fraction. A ten-kroner bill was worth about $2.70, and as for figuring what a ten-ore piece was worth, that got into dividing kroner by ore, a process most of the delegates chose not to attempt for the duration of their stay in Norway.

However, what most severely fazed, and froze the peace pilgrims was that the thermometers never registered a higher temperature than ten degrees below zero. The bare sight of the mercury was enough to send some members into hibernation. However, what they failed to take into account was, as with the ore and kroner, a matter of scale. The Norwegian thermometers were, of course, Centigrade, and the Americans' accustomed Fahrenheit readings would have been all of twenty degrees higher—ten *above*.

The *Studentersamforne*, the great students' Hall of the University of Christiania, opened its doors to a citizens' mass meeting. The hall itself was well-filled with at least a politely interested throng, and many more lined the entrance eager for a glimpse of the famous and controversial leader of the undertaking—Henry Ford himself.

Thereby hung the tale of the whole Expedition, or a crucial part of it. An unscheduled sports event which had been a warm-up to the trek up to *Holmenkollen* was a race between Louis Lochner, Secretary of the Expedition, and the redoubtable Dean Marquis, from the dock to the Grand Hotel. Lochner was armed with a schedule of hotel assignments drawn up by the room committee. According to plan, Ford was to have the middle room of a suite, with his staff member Gaston Plantiff in the bedroom on the right, and Lochner in the bedroom on the left.

However, the eminent divine had outstripped the younger man, and ensconced Ford in a two-room suite, of which the Dean himself and Ford's footman would share the second room, which was the inner one, accessible only through the other, which, as it turned out, was to be kept locked.

Behind the double doors of his own room and that of the reverend, the patron of the Peace Expedition was to languish a virtual prisoner, and in, for the palatial Grand Hotel, a prison-like atmosphere, for it was a northern room. The opalescent northern daylight filtered only dimly through thick curtains, and if the decor had been calculated to depress and deaden the spirits, its gray chill could not have been more effectively contrived.

His sprint on foot to the hotel, and later through the snow-drifts on the mountain sans galoshes, had plunged Ford into a relapse. The flu to which he had fallen victim on board ship after his heavy wetting renewed its hold, and he was confined to his somber quarters with the austere Marquis just at the very inauguration of the Peace Mission.

It fell to Lochner's thankless lot to make the announcement that the man the people had come to see was *hors de combat.* The audience, apparently representative in the main of the local intellectuals, accepted this explanation in good part, and were responsive to the addresses, of which a high point was struck by the imposing Dr. Jenkin Lloyd Jones, who declared, "I belong where the stones are flying." But there was no real ovation, no electric spontaneity.

Ford's absence was a popular disaster in that it was his individual personality, the ambiguous charm which had as its source something in common with their folksy monarch—a naive, unpretentious spirit glorified by the aura of wealth and concomitant power—that had captivated the imagination of Norway.

As for the mission itself, the Norwegian press was fairly united in declaring it useless. Unanimous was praise for the idealism—"a beautiful thing in a world of horror"—and disinterested motives of Ford himself. But Mme. Schwimmer, less able to endear herself, came under criticism for her secretiveness and obtrusiveness in the activities of the Expedition, and opinion prevailed that less could be accomplished under her leadership.

There was also suspicion that the mission was pro-German. The leading paper, the *Aftenposten,* took the stand that no Norwegian delegate should be sent to the Hague conference. Norway herself was pro-Ally. However, the popular stand seemed to be to take the whole thing under advisement until everyone had had a chance to see and hear Ford himself. Thus Ford's personal appearance was a crucial point.

The impression Mme. Schwimmer had created aboard ship was the reverse of the facts. On her foregoing visits to Christiania, according, now, to Government authorities, she had been firmly given to understand that peace efforts at this time were inopportune. Thus any expectation of official recognition was an illusion. And although shipboard announcements had carried the word that efforts would be made to see the king of each nation visited, no such arrangements were instigated in Norway. The official statement was that the mere fact that the delegates were with Ford precluded the possibility. The Christiania press also referred to the delegates as non-representative, declaring that their names meant nothing to Europe, and that there was no plan. The general sentiment seemed to be that the

The bosses of the Expedition.

war should be fought out to its conclusion.

Similarly discouraging were reports from Copenhagen to local papers, indicating that the peace mission would not be well received in Denmark, and that public meetings might even be banned, but this was later retracted.

But many of the pacifists, who, like Dr. Jones, were used to being where the stones were flying, had aspirations for their mission as humble as Rosika's were grandiose. They were happy even to be taken seriously, considering the reaction they had engendered at home and the slapstick trappings with which the embarkation had been invested. Many of the more philosophical among them considered that even the taking of men's minds from slaughter for a time was worth everything. Of course, the "everything" was Ford's; so the pacifists' humility wasn't costing them anything personally.

The American ambassador attended the *Studentersamforne* meeting, with a stenographer who took down the proceedings to forward transcripts to the State Department. He cleared the delegates as "innocuous" and their declarations as "harmless."

The largest of the Norway meetings was held at the *Missions*

Huset, or Missions Hall, with a capacity of about 4,000. The Hall was perhaps three-quarters filled. The speeches were delivered from a pulpit draped in the Norwegian colors. The cavernous hall, with its three tiers of galleries, reminiscent to some of the delegates of the old Madison Square Garden, did not compare favorably in turnout to a typical Garden event. It was at this meeting that Peace Secretary Lochner announced Ford's promise not to leave Norway until he had seen the Norwegians face to face.

The December 22 issue of *Orebladet* paid a personal tribute to Ford and apologized for the "disgusting manner in which a portion of the press of Christiania has dealt with the Expedition." It concluded: "In order that Mr. Ford, whom we esteem most highly because of his philosophy of life, his great idealism, and his warm, noble heart, may not take away from here that Norsemen are nothing but blundering boors, we have in the above placed ourselves on record before his departure."

That departure was to take place in less than twenty-four hours, under circumstances the editor could never have envisioned. Meanwhile, the subject of the tribute was prone in his palatial prison, the Grand Hotel, the ward of the clergy.

Lochner, when he succeeded in penetrating the sickroom, reports that he was "deeply shocked" by Ford's appearance. Not even Lochner's glowing reports of the Norwegian tributes to him brightened Ford's listlessness. He had visibly lost weight in just the three days' time, and his pallor was accentuated by the bleak room. "Guess I had better go home to mother," he said. "I told her I'll be back soon. You've got this thing started now and can get along without me."

Lochner remonstrated. He told Ford that his desertion would discredit the whole Expedition. Ford wavered. Mme. Schwimmer called in a doctor, who diagnosed Ford's illness as genuine enough, but nothing that a week at the health-resort of Finse wouldn't cure. Ford seemed to consider Finse. He told Lochner he would accompany the Expedition at least to Stockholm. To Rosika Schwimmer, who seemed to have something about her that made everybody, even Ford, inclined to discomfit her, he said he was absolutely going home.

In any case, he swore that he would make good his pledge to show himself to the Norwegian people. To a group of Norwegian newsmen whom he received that same evening, he forgot peace and became entirely carried away with a dissertation on the utility of the tractor. He visualized armies of tractors regenerating post-war Europe. He wanted to meet with munitions manufacturers to advise them how to convert to tractor plants. "Swords into plowshares—spears into pruning hooks;" Henry was off again.

9

Peace at Any Price -
or Roughly About a Million

If one militarist, Napoleon, was right about an Army traveling on its stomach, then the Peace Expedition could have rolled. It was not only in the inner spirit that the peace pilgrims were a breed apart from Europe of 1915, but in the inner man.

While the pacifists were partaking of *Kogt Lax m. sauce Hollandaise,* the flavor for middle Europeans was coal-tar. This noble remote ancestor of nylon, coal-tar, the stiff black liquid which is the by-product of burning coal, was first used in the latter Sixteenth century as fuel, and then as a varnish for wood and ropes. A hundred years later it was discovered that through distillation of the coal-tar, various oils could be obtained, the lighter ones being siphoned off first, the heavy next, and the pitch remaining. A new world of synthetics was opened up. Redistillation of the oils and solids ultimately could produce such a range of modern commodities as antiseptics, anaesthetics, aspirin, perfume, saccharin, moth balls, creosote, TNT, tear gas, and photographic developer, to name but a few.

Coal-tar it was that lent its zest to wartime German "coffee," of which the other ingredients were barley and oats. It also provided the base for explosives, dyes, and some 440 other products in medicine, sanitation, and food substitution.

Another elixir of life which spiked the Europeans' "tea" while the Peace Mission and its chroniclers were savoring the wine cellars of the Grand Hotels—every hotel was a "Grand" —was pine bud. The rest of the "tea" was linden blossoms and beech buds. Too generous an admixture of the vital ingredient, pine bud, solved the whole problem by creating a violent emetic.

When the barley and oats ran scarce, the coffee was made of carrots and yellow turnips. "Cocoa" was roasted peas and oats. While the Peace Expedition was eating the real thing ir banquet halls, the people whom they had come to save were consuming ingenious ersatz fabrications, like the rice "lamb chop" with its wooden stick, complete with "pants" for a bone, and the "beef steak" molded of cornmeal, spinach, potatoes and ground nuts, bound with an egg, solid enough to call for a serrated knife.

While Middle and Eastern Europe was contending with the "Iron Ration," Ford took care of his pilgrims. Bed was as well looked after as board—with respect to the material appointments, at least. "This is the royal suite!" cried Henrietta Lindsey, when she and the Judge were shown to their room at the Grand Hotel in Christiania. "There must be some mistake!"

The bedroom was 50 by 22 feet. This was not intended as a delicate—or indelicate— tribute to the judge's advocacy of free love. All the other delegates, the Lindseys were assured, had apartments of equal magnitude.

Not that anybody had roughed it on the Oscar, not even the crew. The tips mounted to almost $5000. Every man in the stoke hole got $10. The chief dining saloon steward was given $500 to divide among the waiters and his bus-boys. No one on the ship was forgotten. At this rate, it is easy to imagine how the expenses of the Expedition had totalled more than $300,000 before it ever landed in Christiania.

Incidentally, Ford had confided to Lochner that he carried $10,000 in cash on his person that not even manager Plantiff knew about, in case he and Lochner should "want to run off on some little stunt of our own."

As one reads this prodigious balance sheet, it should be borne in mind that we are talking about the dollar of 1915—a one-hundred-cents gold dollar, whose purchasing power today would be almost three times as great.

The haphazard and improvised accounting system made it almost impossible to evaluate the daily running expense of the turbulent voyage. In terms of cash, for example, the wireless messages alone had cost Ford well over $10,000. The two wireless operators, who had often worked all night, could testify to the volume of messages, which had broken all the world's records to date for ship-to-shore radiograms. A stenographic report had been taken of everything said in the peace talks—including the students' decision that children ought not to play with tin soldiers. This *process verbaux* was to be set in type later and run off on the press in the smoking saloon on the upper deck, which had been requisitioned for the purpose. It was filled with typewriters, stenographers, multigraphs and dictaphones, and daily handled an amount of correspondence which could not be calculated.

But another passenger paid even more heavily than Henry Ford for the voyage. The wireless messages may have cost Ford $10,000 and more, but for Lloyd Bingham, the ebullient emcee who had perched on the ship's rail at the Hoboken pier to give each boarding celebrity a fitting sendoff, who endeared himself to preparedness and anti-preparedness factions alike with his theater-world's flair for fun, the price came much higher.

Between *mal de mer* and *la grippe*, the Peace Ship was virtually a hospital ship before she was fairly on the high seas, and it was, of course, Ford's condition that caused the greatest consternation. But Bingham's cold soon settled in his lungs. The infection failed to yield to any of the pre-antibiotic era remedies.

Christiania was welcomed now not only as the goal of the peace pilgrimage, but as a source of possible succor for the rapidly sinking Bingham. But when the Oscar came into port, he was carried off the ship in a coma from which he was not to revive.

"I am crazy to go with Henry Ford," Bingham, peacestruck like so many others of the variegated crew, had wired his actress-wife, then performing on tour in Texas. But once out of the aureole of splendor shed by his wife, nothing went right for Bingham, in spite of the fact that he tried to be the life of the peace party—the ship's playboy—until his pneumonia felled him.

And so the round trip promised the pilgrims by Ford was swiftly fulfilled for Bingham, as he had never imagined and now could not know.

And while Bingham was on his deathbed in the Red Cross Hospital and Ford on his sickbed in the vaultlike hotel room, wardened by the vigilant Dean, the delegates set forth to spend $56,000 on a Norwegian "Christmas binge."

Fittingly enough, a golden pig figured prominently in the most brilliant function of the mission's stay in Norway. This was a banquet at the University, of which it was remarked by A. E. Hartzell, who represented both the *Morning* and *Evening Sun* of New York that "the magic touch of gold is expected to turn the tide of popular opinion in Norway in favor of the peace scheme."

Mme. Schwimmer, that one-woman delegation in herself, conceived and carried on her own the notion that a gift of $10,000 be left in every country visited by the Expedition. This proposal gave quite a jolt not only to good company-man Gaston Plantiff, but to Henry Ford himself, who, as usual on this trip, was the last to know how generous he had been. Since the University students were collecting funds for a commons, or club house, this seemed a golden opportunity for the 14-karat touch of the peace mission to manifest itself.

The Norwegians, who had remained politely aloof from the pacifists' message, went wild over the munificence. When Lochner announced that Henry Ford had become the first donor to the clubhouse fund, an ovation made it impossible for the President of the Association even to make his thanks heard for more than twenty minutes.

During his official speech of appreciation, four students approached Plantiff, as the representative of Henry Ford, bearing on their shoulders a life-sized gilded pig, which was made to bow solemnly several times.

The symbolism of ancient Norse mythology, in which the pig is esteemed as a vehicle of gratitude and comfort, eluded some of the earthier elements of the American press, which, hearing about this ceremony, had considerable sport with "His Majesty the Pig" and "His Pigship."

Meanwhile, a news cartoon depicted Ford on his sickbed remarking, "Hope I'll be out of the hospital by Christmas." But a Michigan paper went farther. In one of those crazy headlines which characterized many of the news stories emanating from the Ford Peace Expedition, a Dearborn paper proclaimed in bold type: "Ford Dead!"

While the delegates were doing Christiania in taxis to the tune of $2,000 in cab fares, what was going on in the back bedroom where the sponsor was missing all the fun?

It was on the evening of December 23, having given his word to the people of Norway that he would make a public appearance, that Ford found himself wrestling with his own soul. Of what went on that night, Marquis, in his biography of Ford, remains silent, although he describes in detail his travail with Ford the night before the Oscar II sailed.

We tried most of the night to prevail on him to abandon

the trip. His reply to me was, "It is right to try to stop war, isn't it?" To this I could only reply—yes. "Well," he would go on, "you have told me what is right cannot fail."

The Dean goes on to describe how he labored to explain to Ford that one cannot do what is "right" in the *wrong* way. To do what is right, the right means have to be used. Ford would not make any direct reply to this. He wasn't up to a theological debate with the churchman. Instead, he only reiterated that he had a "hunch" about what he was doing.

The Dean could get nowhere with him—nowhere, that is, in the realm of abstract reasoning, at least, not then. But Marquis was willing to bide his time. He would get through to Ford if he had to cross the ocean, and this he did. The Dean never made any bones about his motives. It was his design to catch Ford in a vulnerable moment, pry him from his commitment to the Expedition, and pack him back home. It was this mission of moral sabotage that put Marquis in the same boat with such stalwarts of peace as Schwimmer and Lochner.

It was the night before Christmas and all through the hotel—the Grand Hotel at 2 a.m., in fact—a group of delegates sat around debating what their sponsor might actually do. A report came that something was going on in the Ford suite. Between 3 and 4 a.m. on Christmas Eve, Ford's footman was seen carrying out a trunk. Surely Henry was not playing Santa Claus at that hour, albeit he had been rehearsing the role since he left Hoboken!

Mme. Schwimmer roused the whole hotelful of delegates. Those who were up singing Christmas carols and drinking *glogg* were detailed to waken others. Plantiff himself seemed to feel betrayed by this surreptitious departure of his boss. "The old man lied to me, that's what he did! He told me he wouldn't leave till the morning." Ford, of course, had not said what time in the morning.

The hotel lobby was in an uproar as the peace delegates tried to remonstrate with Ford as he was escorted by the Dean to the waiting taxi. "Go ahead!" Marquis shouted to the driver the moment they were fairly inside the cab, and so they swirled off into the snowy darkness of the Norwegian dawn.

But the bereft delegates were left with one gratification. Bedeviled and pilloried by newsmen throughout the Expedition, now, at the moment of denouement which the reporters had been thirsting for, the peace pilgrims were without a leader, indeed, but at least without journalist predators, either. Most of them had stayed in bed.

It was a moment of truth all round.

It had been none other than Henry Ford's own bodyguard who had tipped off Mme. Schwimmer. He had let her in on the news that Ford's baggage had gone to the railroad station, and that its owner would soon follow. Why did he inform on his employer? It was due to a guilty conscience. The young bodyguard had previously pulled a "dirty job" on La Schwimmer. It had been his assignment on board the Oscar to spy on her. His specific detail was to sit up all night watching her door and Ford's, to make sure that no one went from one to the other.

There was a fine irony in this. It had been almost an aberration of the Hungarian feminist that she was beset by spies. "They are watching me!" was always her attitude. They were watching indeed. It was another case of a neurotic fear being fully validated.

Rosika would have been even more dismayed had she been aware that the little black bag she took with her everywhere had been investigated down to its very last rip in the lining of its back compartment.

It had happened one day that an emergency false alarm had been rung aboard ship—and in her haste to clamber out of her room, she had given Ford's man the golden opportunity of a peek into the coveted brief.

The dedicated Rosika, who seemed to do nothing but breathe, eat, sleep and think peace negotiations, had in her famous mystery bag neither cloak nor dagger, nor the "secret

ENOUGH IS ENOUGH!

T. E. POWERS, INTERNATIONAL NEWS SERVICE.

papers" some suspected. What turned up, much to the surprise of Ford's snoop, was a stack of mishmash to attest to the other side of Rosika—her purely feminine person. There were, in addition to her wallet and passport: miniature perfume vials; cleansing tissue and cream; a big kit of facial cosmetics with tweezer; a packet of photos of her loved ones; souvenir post cards; an appointment book; a miniature calendar; an address book; a diary (which described the personalities on Oscar II with good-natured wit); a miniature deck of cards; a package of Sen-Sen; a small dictionary; two white lace handkerchiefs; old receipts; and a small shaker of baby powder.

This image of Rosika was that of a typical subscriber to a ladies' home journal. Never again, once word got out about the contents of the little black bag, did anyone fear this accessory which had seemed to irritate so many.

The emotional Plantiff reported himself quite unmanned by a chance reunion with his boss at the railway station, where Ford and his Peace Party were in separate trains, bound in opposite directions. "Honestly," said Plantiff, afterwards, "I bawled like a child. He kissed me like a father would. I shall never forget the look in his eyes."

"Ford Quits in Fear of Assassin" read the Norwegian headlines. The story went that one of the peace "evangels," disgruntled since the preparedness dispute on the Oscar, had been lying in wait with a loaded revolver outside Ford's room at the Grand Hotel in Christiania, and Ford prudently had bided his time to escape the overwrought pacifist.

The last laugh, as far as the basic commodity went, was enjoyed by the delegates. Plantiff discovered just in time that the letter of credit left him by Ford would have expired by December 31, leaving the party stranded there near the Arctic Circle. An urgent cable to the bank in Detroit extended the credit for another month and another $100,000.

It should not be forgotten that Ford's invitation carried with it the assumption of a round trip to Europe, though not one single mention had ever been made about a legal—a contractual-stipulation to bring everyone back to America. The credit extension, at the very least, assured the company that there would be enough funds for the return voyage.

The boss was already en route home. He had to go to Bergen, on the tip of snow-covered Europe, to board the S.S. *Bergensfjord* for "home and mother." Also going back to "home and mother" was the messenger boy, Jake Greenberg, and a coffin containing the remains of Lloyd Bingham. For all three the historic house-party had ended.

Meanwhile, Stockholm, the next stop of the deserted pilgrims, was reading in the *Tagbladet* its own version of the story behind Ford's departure. And now, with ardor and money to burn, the pilgrims primed themselves to storm Sweden, where, the Norwegians warned them, everybody stayed home for Christmas.

10

Running Wild on Ford's Dough

"The coldest ride in history" was the way one delegate put it. Napoleon's trek through Russia was salubrious by comparison. At any rate, it is unrecorded that any other convention on wheels ever took its course so near the North Pole as that in the eleven railway cars, conspicuously placarded for identification like a circus train, which bore the delegates on the first leg of their land pilgrimage. And while they went about breaking records, it must also have heartened the pacifists to know that the night they rode from Christiania to Stockholm was the coldest in one hundred thirty years.

The rest of Christiania slept deep under quilts as the porters tramped through the corridors of the Grand and its neighboring hotels, rousing the delegates at 6 a.m. The pacifists got up to find the steam radiators frozen and thick ice cakes on their water pitchers. That sentinel of most of their Scandinavian sojourn, the almost omnipresent moon, shone brightly in through the windows. The delegates from California found this early-morning ordeal especially severe.

A number of the pilgrims still had a touch of the flu hanging on, and trooped down to breakfast in wool hose, overcoats and mufflers, clutching bottles of cough syrup. While the steaming Norwegian hot chocolate sent reactive shudders of comfort through their chilled bodies, the delegates went through elaborate calculations with *ore* and dollars once more, to determine the tips to be left to the porters.

The scheduled train-time was 8:30 a.m. However, the severity of the cold made it necessary to thaw out the engine, and that, plus the heating of the cars and clearing of the tracks of the heavy snow, took two hours. The peace party members tried to crowd into the waiting room which was swept by icy winds each time the door was opened, and they stamped and flailed arms in an effort to keep their circulations going. When the Henry Ford Peace Expedition train was finally called, a great cheer went up.

But inside the train, which resembled one of the miniatures run at amusement parks, it was soon discovered that the rear cars, which were occupied by women delegates and correspondents as well as by men, were completely unheated.

Rosika Schwimmer, always bent on improving each shining hour, whether of daylight or moonlight, was surrounded in her car by her typewriters, multigraphs, dictaphones and secretaries, and went right on where she had left off in the Grand Hotel. But it might be noted that her car was comfortably heated, while those of such distinguished delegates as Judge and Mrs. Lindsey, the Rev. and Mrs. Jenkin Lloyd Jones, Mary Fels and May Wright Sewall, were like freezer compartments. During the night the venerable Dr. Jones wandered from compartment to compartment in search of blankets, of which there were none. The newsreel camera men diverted themselves by coasting on a sliding pond in the passageway just outside the glass doors of the compartment, but most took to more conventional bracers, and a number of abstainers waived the pledge for the duration.

A young woman delegate fiddled to the vocal accompani-

ment of members who had discovered both brandy and a voice.
Even the Rev. Theolopsis Montgomery undertook to cheer one
and all with repeated and profoundly earnest renditions of
"Sweet Adeline." The refrain to all the vocalizing was "Send
the bill to Gaston Plantiff."

Then there was a period of panic when Judge Lindsey disappeared. Delegates attempting to snatch forty winks were
rudely roused by one of the Ford stenographers rushing
through the train, paging Judge Lindsey at the top of his lungs.
Some theorized that the Judge had fallen off the train, others
that he had never gotten on it. Innocent strangers to the Judge
who had succeeded, between the cold and the brandy, in
slipping into brief somnolence were pummeled violently awake
with train cushions and dragged out into the light to be asked,
"Is that you, Judge Lindsey?"

When he was almost given up for missing somewhere in
Sweden, the Judge was found in one of the forward compartments, where it was warmer. He was no sooner retrieved than
the correspondents wished he would get lost again, particularly
when he insisted upon grabbing the emergency stop cord every
time he wanted to call a porter.

The night was well worn on when Plantiff, who kept picking
up all the tabs, managed to fall into a doze. This respite was
short-lived. Ford's man had barely slipped into heaven knows
what dreams or nightmares when the lamp in his compartment
exploded and the flames threatened to sweep the train. The
crew was called in to put out the fire, and Plantiff sat up for the
rest of the night.

Tributes to their late comrade Lloyd Bingham and the official announcement of Henry Ford's retirement from the Expedition further dampened spirits, and it was a train-soiled, bone-
chilled and subdued phalanx of peace pilgrims that bore down
upon Stockholm at a dark 9:30 in the morning, with only a few
delegates exhilarated by the climate—and they were from

Charge It to Hennery

By T. E. Powers, the Famous Cartoonist

Copyright, 1915, by the Star Company. Great Britain Rights Reserved.

T. E. POWERS, INTERNATIONAL NEWS SERVICE.

North Dakota. By eleven the caravan arrived at the luxurious Grand Hotel.

It has been fashionable—and accurate—to portray these traditional European Grand Hotels, their lobbies, their restaurants and bars and royal suites, as points of convergence for the cloak-and-dagger set of both sides in the global conspiracy—yesterday's and today's—and Stockholm was Europe's deluxe center of international intrigue. The Mata Haris and James Bonds of an earlier era were swarming over the public halls of the Stockholm Grand in a veritable eisteddfod of spies, counterspies, propagandists, military attaches, oil men, munitions salesmen, black marketeers, journalists and—demi and quarter mondaines who didn't care where their next mink came from.

On this sophisticated and somewhat sinister stage, without cue or make-up, walked the delegation of Fordites—innocents abroad and untutored in the mores of fraternization with secret agents. When the Ford party arrived with their carload of luggage, every lounge chair in the foyer was occupied. A gallery of spying eyes, sheltered behind unfolded newspapers bearing mastheads in a score of languages, was taking in every detail —scrutinizing, analyzing, gauging and evaluating every face, piece of luggage and manner of dress. By evening of that first day this conglomeration of mid-west accents, provincial raiment and evangelical mien had been written off as an inoffensive, undefiled, lamb-like covey of pilgrims. There was no visible corruption, no glamor, no pay-dirt for the secret agent community. Only a few of the newspapermen and their goodlooking wives, dressed in the best from New York's Siegel-Cooper, rated so much as an undistracted glance.

The sub-zero rigors of the trip quickly faded from their thoughts as the delegates were once more ensconced in a Grand Hotel; this was one of the most splendid in all of Europe, its neoclassic patio redolent of hyacinths, hydrangeas, palms, Christmas greens and hot rumors.

Every aspect of that Christmas Eve was perfect—on the great canal which flowed with swift current between the royal palace and the Grand Hotel with the green calcium lights on its roof, ducks and swans rode along the streams on ice cakes. Sleds passed along the avenue with bells jingling. Taxis—or drosches, as they were called here—stood in snow to the wheel hubs. Quiet snow had been falling steadily for days in such Christmas weather as Scandinavia revels in. Inside their firelit homes, the Swedish families decorated their trees with apples and candles in the scent of roasting goose, and sang "Silent Night" and "A Mighty Fortress is Our God," in Swedish, of course.

But the fairytale-like surroundings did little to pick up the spirits of the delegates, despondent over Ford's desertion and thoughts of loved ones back home in the States. A Mississippi publisher told the gathering that he had just cabled his printers (on Ford's dough, naturally), to tell them he wished he were there. An aged delegate from Illinois talked about his grandchildren, and even a New York reporter broke up at the orchestra's playing of "Oh Where and Oh Where Has my Highland Laddie Gone," because it reminded him of his adopted little boy home in New York. When the orchestra played "America," the entire body of two hundred men and women rose as one and sang it as, no doubt, none of them ever had in their lives before.

But it was not all shivering and *schmalz* for the peace troupe in Scandinavia. As Christmas morning dawned, the delegates found new accord in one regard at least—that Sweden really was for them. Although it was true that the Swedish Christmas was normally celebrated in the bosom of the family, so exclusively that shops, hotels and public affairs of all kinds are shut down, Stockholm outdid itself in the fervor of its welcome to the peace party.

All were aware that Sweden had to perform her thankless traditional role of the pre-eminently neutral country—feeding a starving, blockaded Germany, and sustaining a number of agencies dedicated to the aid of war victims. Fulfilling the onerous task of heading that Swedish government was the lot of a quiet, aristocratic, political figure named Hjalmar Hammarskjöld, who was apologetic about his inability to "officially" receive and fraternize with the American peace delegates. Yet, in a moment of conviviality, when his impartial guard was down, he uttered a phrase which was to be given some emphasis 45 years later by his son in a conversation in New York. Dag Hammarskjöld, the late Secretary General of the United Nations, who was an adolescent when the Ford party came to Stockholm, repeated his father's utterance: "It is important for

Sweden to be neutral, but neutral on the right side."

Now the Swedish program of the Expedition got formally under way with a Yuletide ceremony in the Odeon at eight o'clock in the morning, with socialist *Borgmastare* (Mayor) Lindhagen, saluting the delegates with "It has been your will and desire to contribute your quota, from a new quarter and in a new mode, to the output of spiritual munitions of peace, which all in good time are destined to expel even stupidity from its fortified entrenchments."

At last the pacifists felt they were among people who, spiritually if not literally, spoke their language. Rounds of mass-meetings and testimonial dinners followed, and even the American ambassador was genial, while emphasizing that these acts of friendship were "unofficial."

Hardly less than by the pacific rapport with the Swedes were the delegates charmed by Stockholm's "automats." Such was the delight of the American temper with the arrangement whereby one might stick a ten-ore piece in the slot, put a glass under the spigot, and watch the hot and heady brew, *glogg*, rush in, that many repeated the process until, as one correspondent put it, they felt competent to take the Government post office and relocate it on the next block.

This device, enabling people to buy a bender from a machine, moved one delegate to contemplations of poetic drift:

> Life is profitless and flat
> Without a Swedish automat.
>
> A drosche stood upon the spec,
> Eating ore by the peck.

Of course the conveniences of Stockholm were not without their price, but this was not the delegates' worry. In fact, one of the Expedition parlor games was to see who could run up the highest bill. It may have been in this ambition that one correspondent, whose firewood delivery to his room was delayed, solved the fuel problem by disjointing the chairs and sticking

The Ford Peace Party, Stockholm 1916.

the arms and legs into the stove. The resulting bill probably represented close to the highest heating cost in history. Other guests might have had similar recourse to their furnishings, except that the Swedish porcelain stoves were difficult to identify as such, looking more like mantelpieces or pier glasses.

A lesser bit of vandalism was inadvertently perpetrated by one of the motion picture men, who spattered a little ink on a rug that might have cost $18 at Sears and Roebuck. The damage bill was such that he felt moved to validate it somewhat by cutting the rug into small pieces. Another delegate presented the Ford Transportation Bureau with a bill for 100 kroner— about $20—for getting his suit pressed because he had to sit up all night on the train.

These financial details were easily deposited on the Ford outfit's doorstep; but the delegates did encounter small personal problems with the language. The Swedes, unlike the Norwegians, frequently could not say so much as "Good morning" in English. One delegate, in a vain effort to cable his wife "Merry Christmas" was directed first to the fifth floor of the King's palace. His second try for information in a jewelry shop was responded to with a tray of watches. Finally he went into a bank and addressed his inquiry to a woman teller, who rushed behind a metal gate, barred it, and screamed "Go away!" Like a bona fide bank robber, the peace pilgrim made a fast getaway, jolted out of his Yule spirit.

The total cost of the Ford Peace adventure has actually never been established on a dollar and cents accounting sheet. Fantastic sums ranging from one to five million dollars have been mentioned by the uninformed across the years. During the decade following the end of the Expedition, disclosures about costly items which were not part of the original "cost sheet" have come to light. Such items as gifts of some twenty Ford cars to important European figures kept popping up and were neither confirmed nor denied by the "management" in charge of money. No one has ever been able, for example, to estimate how much money was pocketed in kick-backs, rake-offs, and other illegitimate payoffs connected with goods, services and transportation sold to the Expedition. Since no itemized account was ever published, the guessing soared with the passing years.

At one point, years ago, Louis Lochner did obtain a figure which added up to some $400,000. Using this as a basis, Lochner did some fascinating figuring.

"Assuming," he said, "that Ford's total worth at that time was not less than $150,000,000, the Expedition cost him less than one twentieth of a year's interest on his capital." Supposing his millions bear six per cent interest, Henry Ford's money, without a stroke of work on his part, within sixteen days after he had started from New York, had already "earned" the entire cost of the Expedition with all its extravagances, with all its "extras." Let us remember: there were no tax deductions for his do-good enterprises—but then, let's face it, there were virtually no taxes. The extravagance—and there was much of it—was by no means primarily due to a reckless desire to have a good time at someone else's expense. Henry Ford himself had again and again stated that "money was no object," that he had dedicated his life *and his fortune* to the stoppage of war, that he "would back the Women's International Committee to the last dollar."

As already noted, the lobby of the Grand Hotel was the most picturesque spot in all Stockholm, a kind of all-hours club of the most cosmopolitan personages that might be met with anywhere in Europe. Conspicuous among them was an elegant lieutenant who wore a monocle. (It created a sensation among the Americans, for few had ever seen one except on Leo Dichtrichstein in a Molnar play). The lieutenant also had a delicate feather of a mustache, and a sheer handkerchief in his sleeve. He produced instantly upon introduction a card elaborately engraved with a baronial coat of arms and the name

"Gösta Liewan Stierngranat." Lieutenant Stierngranat was an aristocrat to the teeth, with a tendency to challenge to the field of honor any critic of monarchy.

Unfortunately for the lieutenant's chivalric concepts, his chief challenger was a lady, one of the more vigorous and strong-lunged exponents of the common man among the Expedition's energetic bluestockings. Lieutenant Stierngranat tried to outpace his female opponent in the palatial corridors, but she proved she could stride as fast as he, skirts and all. After a confrontation on the subject of the Lusitania, during which the lady-pacifist's arguments evoked echoes from the coffers of the ceiling, the Lieutenant retired from the thickly-carpeted field of battle with all the dignity he could muster, and engaged the weaker sex no more during the pacifist visitation.

Another equally remarkably turned-out frequenter of the lobby proved more genially disposed. Since he did not offer his card, his unpronounceable first name remained in doubt, and he was rechristened by the correspondents "Scrooge" Patursson.

"Scrooge" was first observed lounging in the lobby with one finger propped pensively against his chin, and his eyes rolled up in contemplation of the ceiling. By the length of his hair, he was first presumed a European delegate; but it turned out that he was the editor of a small newspaper. The hair, which overhung his eyes, apparently had served him throughout the Swedish winters in lieu of a hat, since his birth in the Faro Islands. He had no collar, either, but compensated for this richly with a sky-blue waistcoat adorned with thirteen silver buttons and fastened at the top with a silver crown. Over this he wore a black velvet bolero with jet buttons the size of silver dollars. His knickers were made of doeskin, terminating in black stockings and thick-soled tan shoes.

The correspondents took elated possession of "Scrooge" and besought him to come to America.

"Patursson, we've named a city in New Jersey after you," one newsman encouraged him.

"Yes?" said Scrooge, gratified.

"Wait till the great impresario Frank Bostock gets hold of you," another correspondent blandished him. "On Broadway you'll get it coming and going."

"First I learn English?" suggested Scrooge.

"That's unnecessary," said the newsmen.

Flattered, Scrooge undertook to return the correspondents' hospitality handsomely by teaching them the native folk dances of the Faro Islands. While a correspondent played the concert grand piano, Scrooge hopped up and down the salon in a rhythmic skip, flapping his arms like the wings of a seagull. Imitating his solemnity, the newsmen joined him in skipping and flapping, while over the scene glared the state portrait of the late King Oscar, resplendent in his uniform and decorations.

A crowd quickly collected to view the spectacle of American newsmen, flushed with unaccustomed exertion, hopping and beating their ribs with their elbows under the vigorous tutelage of the Faro Islander. As if out of the polished woodwork they came, spy and counterspy, all the mysterious meanderers who haunted the lobby, and the peace delegates.

It broke up the correspondents. One of them started laughing, and hilarity swept the folk-dancers. For the first time it hit home to Scrooge that this was all a joke to his new-found American friends, that he, too, was a joke. He stopped leading the dancing, pulled himself together, and walked out of the salon without a word or look around. Their clown had left the ring, but the convulsed newsmen couldn't stop laughing.

This was the occasion that the fastidious Lieutenant of the monocle, mustache, and embroidered handkerchief in the uniform-sleeve, showed that he was an aristocrat in more than his elegance and penchant for monarchy. Or perhaps his own total rout at the hands of the vociferous lady delegate, who had proved she could out-shout and out-pace him, had awakened his fellow-feeling. He followed Scrooge out of the salon, and presently brought him back. The tables were turned. The dancers sobered down and sobered up, and the two countrymen, blueblood and peasant, had the final triumph. They had enacted for the "pacifists" the meaning of reconciliation.

All the festivities and frolicking going on below-stairs never reached the ears of Rosika Schwimmer, who was closeted with the most serious delegates, Frederick Holt, civic leader of Detroit, and with his independently active philanthropic wife, and Louis Lochner, and Mary Fels, the organizer of many foundations and philanthropies and the wife of Joseph Fels, the Philadelphia millionaire maker of Fels Naptha soap. Fels, at that time, had more money than Henry Ford.

"We have conquered Sweden," Holt remarked. "Our reception has exceeded our fondest expectations. The idea is taking hold."

"The high spot of our pilgrimage," Lochner calls the Swedish sojourn. "Nowhere," he wrote, "was there a more sympathetic understanding of our aims and objectives than among these modern descendants of the Vikings."

In fact, the Swedes indicated their desire to extend their hospitality to the pacifists indefinitely. Stockholm's Mayor Lindhagen formally invited the Expedition to adopt his city instead of The Hague as permanent home of the Continuous Mediation Conference—the ultimate aim of the Expedition, and it was at this time that the idea was first given serious consideration. Meanwhile, all the inchoate and grandiose plans of the Expedition were being hammered and shaped into workable, viable form. Mme. Schwimmer didn't even take time off from the vast organizational job to go down to meals.

Of the many functions set up in Stockholm for the Peace Expedition, which drew more than twice the attendance of those in Norway, one crowning event was the public meeting at the

The Vacillating Sons of St. Vitus: upper row: Arthur E. Hartzell, *N.Y. Sun;* Marian Rubicam, *Collier's;* Helen Lowry, *N.Y. Post;* Elmer Davis, *N.Y. Times;* William C. Bullitt, *Philadelphia Ledger;* Ted Pockman, *N.Y. Tribune;* S. S. McClure. Middle: Berton Braley, *Collier's;* Joseph Jefferson O'Neill, *N.Y. World;* Scrooge Patursson; Inez Mulholland Boissevain; Maxwell Swain, *N.Y. Herald;* Carolyn Wilson, *Chicago Tribune.* Lower: J. Bayne, Fox Newsreel; Burnet Hershey; Charles "Perky" Stewart, United Press.

Academy of Music. Although the Swedish temper at this time was rather pro-German than emotionally neutral, acclaim was tumultuous on the part of the normally undemonstrative citizenry. "Nothing like this has ever been seen in Scandinavia" was the verdict of natives and American residents alike. Sweden had gone overboard for the peace pilgrims.

Yet fourth-estate skulduggery continued unabated. When Lochner got back to the hotel from the scene of the triumph, he was shown a hotel-desk blotter, discovered at 5 p.m., three hours before the meeting took place, bearing a single imprint. Advised to hold it up to a mirror to read it, he was amazed to distinguish the text of a dispatch reading in part "Mass meeting

THE GOLDEN DOVE OF PEACE!

T. E. POWERS, INTERNATIONAL NEWS SERVICE.

Academy of Music tonight a failure. One krone admission
frightened thrifty Stockholm folk away."

Win or lose, the pacifists couldn't hope, it seemed, for a good
review on the part of the reporter who had repaid Ford's exclusive interview by reporting the magnate chained to his bunk.

For the culminating event of their stay in Sweden, the banquet at the sumptuous Grand Hotel, with its colonnades, chan-
deliers, and tree-high potted palms, full dinner dress was
obligatory.

This was a requirement posing a delicate problem for this reporter. In Europe, the formal amenities were not available on a
transient basis, and nowhere could one rent a dinner jacket. I
canvassed a few European neighbors at the Hotel and the U.S.
Consul himself. The only offer anyone came up with was a suit
that might have served me as a four-man tent.

In despair of getting in to the banquet for want of basic sar-
torial credentials, I tried to forget the whole thing by going to
the theater. The show was a routine, bouncy German operetta,
complete with the soprano with flat, flaxen braids, geraniums,
tankards, carved clocks, and a duke. Something about the duke
caught my wandering attention, and began to appeal to me
strangely, and it was not his voice.

He was wearing a dinner jacket, and he was just my size.

Before the last curtain had been called, I was backstage
negotiating feverishly with the surprised tenor-duke. By emphasizing that my future as a journalist and the peace of Europe were at stake, I managed to conclude the deal and get the
crucial regalia on the strict terms that I would get it back to
the theater the next day in time for the matinee.

At the banquet table, rich funereal fumes arose around me
over the aroma of the *Pochered Sparrisfylld fiskrulad au vin
blanc* and the *Brakt Farsklax a la Doria*. Months of greasepaint
had permeated my borrowed splendor, and I smelled like a
star's dressing room. Afterwards, I learned that everybody else
had gone out and bought everything he needed and charged it

to Plantiff. By my economy, or ignorance, I cut expenses in Sweden by $50—the current price of a ready-to-wear dinner coat.

The night of the departure from Stockholm, Scrooge Patursson haunted the hotel lobby. From his meager funds he had invested in a bouquet of hothouse flowers, presenting each lady delegate with a blossom until he ran out of floral tributes.

Fifteen hundred Swedes turned out at the railroad station to see the pilgrims off. The Working Men's Male Chorus serenaded them alternately with American songs and thrillingly massive Scandinavian choruses. Not to let this golden opportunity slip, one after another of the more prominent delegates appeared on the train platform to make a final speech, and amid the *halsningars* of their Swedish friends, the train of pacifists began to pull out.

As the delegates in the forward cars were singing "America," a single figure loomed up out of the crowd on the station platform, waving his arms wildly. "Great America! Great America!" Those were the only words Scrooge Patursson had learned to say clearly.

Banquet in Stockholm.

11

Publicity Stunt or Crusade?

First of all, it should be clarified that between publicity and public service there was no essential split in Ford's thinking, as there was none in his life. He could not really separate his integrity from his "image" any more than a Hollywood personality might in a later day, or, for that matter, than any business magnate then or now.

The public-relations expert, Edward L. Bernays, has pointed out that the whole concept of public relations and of "created circumstances" was unknown in 1915. Bernays himself believes that Ford was an essentially simple man of action, given to dynamic responses which might be triggered by the most offhand suggestion. Bernays recalls that at the time of Light's Golden Jubilee in 1929, he noticed an empty lot in Greenfield Village at Dearborn, and remarked to Ford, "There should be some grass." Ford grabbed the phone, said, "Get me Liebold," and ordered his secretary, "Liebold, get that field at Greenfield Village planted with turf immediately." (Bernays does not, of course, know how Liebold took this, but having lived through the trans-ocean planting of seeds of peace, the secretary may have considered planting some seeds of grass a pleasure.)

Bernays notes an instinctive recognition in Ford of the dramatic contrast between the "trenches" and "Christmas." And the slogan "Out of the trenches by Christmas!" the public-relations master explains, had impact because it stated the objective dramatically and specifically. The appraisal seems general that Ford had "a feeling" for things, or as he himself would have said, "a hunch." If he always knew exactly what he was doing, it was on this instinctual level, not the calculating one.

Business was Ford's life, although by the American heritage, unconsciously potent in his motivations, and in vindication of the scale to which he developed it, he had to euphemize it as work. The concept of *work* was one of his prime philosophies. *"The natural thing to do is to work . . . I take it for granted that we must work . . . There is plenty of work to do. Business is merely work . . . It is work and work alone that can deliver the goods . . . The moral fundamental is man's right in his labor . . . through work and work alone may health, wealth, and happiness inevitably be secured . . . money comes naturally as the result of service . . . business exists for service."*

In 1915, this man who worshipped work, entering his second half-century, must occasionally have sensed that his real work was done. By his own convictions, this would have vitiated him as a man. Naturally, instead of allowing any let-up, Ford's work began multiplying in all directions.

Ford's forty-years' associate and biographer, Charles Sorensen, sees the Peace Ship as the first explosion of a chain reaction. Soon to follow it was the development of "one of the wonders of the modern industrial world," the fantastic River Rouge empire. But by its own inner momentum, Ford's "work" could not be contained by a mere industrial empire. This was the point at which it began to branch out. He got involved not only in the international scene, but in domestic politics. He tried to formulate a kind of Fordian systematic theology of the trinity of work, free enterprise, and service. What he believed and what was good for business were inextricably tied up together.

The American passion for grand scale was preeminent in Ford. With regard to an often-noted personal modesty and humility, it may be only the other side of the same coin that Ford saw as he felt himself as something of a giant among men. His life was his own interpretation, probably unconscious, of the parable of the talents—"From whom to whom much is given, much shall be required." There is no more telling passage in Ford's personal testament than his assertion of the inequality of man.

> There can be no greater absurdity and no greater dis-service to humanity in general than to insist that all men are equal. Most certainly all men are not equal, and any democratic conception which strives to make men equal is only an effort to block progress. Men cannot be of equal service. The men of larger ability are less numerous than the men of smaller ability; it is possible for a mass of the smaller men to pull the larger ones down—but in so doing they pull themselves down. It is the larger men who give the leadership to the community and enable the smaller men to live with less effort.

It is significant that Ford's comment on Wilson should have been "He's a small man."

Ford thought big in every sense, and an idea as big as an ocean liner was just his size. Misgivings about vulgarity which made such finer-grained peace-recruits from the great world of letters and social service as Jane Addams squeamish could not have occurred to Ford any more than to a modern ad-man. If peace was the end, publicity was the means, and it is inevitable that the interrelationship herein be scrutinized. But it ought to be remembered that the Ford Motor Company had a "Social Services" division long before a promotion department became a rule-of-thumb setup in church and non-profit organizations. Ford was a pioneer, by nature both inborn and acquired.

As for the vaudeville ramifications which the ship idea was presently to take on, to an age conditioned by Chatauquas where productions of *Godefroi and Yolande* and sermons by William Jennings Bryan vied with male choruses gotten up in camisoles, feather boas, bustles and garters, the discrepancy of mood between mission and accouterments was not grotesque —not any more so than the contrast between photographs of riots, freaks and movie sets in present-day weekly magazines is to us.

If his ship became a joke even before she sailed, Ford had sound precedent for counting this as a possible asset. The Ford automobile had chalked up plenty of mileage on enough Ford-jokes to pave the roads, or to fill a book—and two books of them actually were compiled. Ford jokes took practically every form.

> "My father is crazy over his Ford."
> "Whenever I see him, he's crazy under it."

> "Do you know Detroit?"
> "Sure. That's where they make automobiles."
> "They make other things there, too."
> "I know. I rode in one."

Then there was the anecdote variety: A New Yorker on one of the Ford Motor Company's inspection tours for visitors happened to meet with Henry Ford personally, who remarked to him, "That car has exactly 4,719 parts." Later, talking with one of the engineers, the visitor asked lightly if there were actually 4,719 parts in that model. "I'm sure I don't know," said the engineer. "And I can't think of a more useless piece of information." There were Ford metaphors—"as nervous as a jellyfish on a Ford fender."

But, as another Ford joke went, while the country was laughing at Henry Ford's car, he himself was getting real fun out of another machine—an adding machine. Ford had the figures on what all the jokes added up to, and when it came to a venture in another field, he was not only placid about the jibes, but complacent. Of Ford jokes of his personal authorship—"I drive an English car instead of a Ford when I'm on vacation and don't care if I get anywhere"—we have seen that he tried softening up President Wilson with one when he sought official backing for his ship.

But if there had been intended any secondary use of the Peace Ship to sell cars instead of peace, there are facts that speak for themselves. A signal milestone in the story of the Ford Motor Company was to pass while the great man himself deliberately absented himself, so that the full commercial value of the event could not be exploited. On December 10, 1915, the millionth Ford car was to roll off the assembly line, and Ford was on the high seas. With only two weeks to the deadline for his new product—peace—he couldn't wait in Detroit. But asked if he really expected to get the boys out of the trenches by Christmas, Ford contributed to the ship-jokes himself, in the Ford tradition: "Well, there's always Easter, and the Fourth of July."

Not only did Ford willingly miss out on the big day at his plant, but his outspoken peace views cost him advertising. The British newspapers turned down his layouts. As we have seen, his pacifism also cost Ford his vice-president, but it is true that Couzens had pretty much outlived his usefulness.

Of the depth of his pacifist convictions, Ford's own writings can scarcely leave reasonable doubt. Seven years after his Peace Expedition, he wrote, "Today I am more opposed to war than I ever was, and I think the people of the world know— even if the politicians do not—that war never settles anything." He blamed war for reducing the orderly and profitable processes of the world to "a loose, disjointed mass." He noted that war makes some poor, and makes some rich, but that those who get rich get rich safe at home. He said that no patriotic man could bear to make money out of war and out of human life. He said that not until mothers make money by losing their sons on the battlefield should a citizen consent to make money "out of providing his country with the means to preserve its life."

In his decrying of war profiteers, Ford, who feared a mysterious "creeping Orientalism" taking over American life, unquestionably rose to radical heights of eloquence: "There is a power within the world which cries 'War!' and in the confusion of the nations, the unrestrained sacrifice which people make for safety and peace runs off with the spoils of the panic."

He believed that the essential point to keep in mind was that the world, though winning a war, did not win over the promotors of war. He called war a manufactured evil, fostered by definite techniques. Suspicion between nations is fostered by "a press whose interest is locked up with the interests that will be benefited by war." "Then the 'overt act' will appear. It is no trick at all to get an 'overt act' once you work the hatred of two nations up to the proper pitch." "War, is an orgy of money, just as it is an orgy of blood."

Finally, it should be recalled that just as the Peace Ship was to embark, Ford suffered qualms, and asked if he might personally withdraw, while still footing the bill. His personal demeanor was recessive throughout. He was obviously fazed by the fanfare. He didn't want to make speeches. He was also afraid of the winter sea, the ruthless U-boats, but even more than anything else, of a scornful opinion painting him as a "coward" or worse, a "welcher."

Possibly the accusations that Ford's motives were not disinterested were fostered by Ford's own wry comment: "Best free advertising I ever got." Some of his subsequent comments on his Peace Ship sounded crass. "If we had tried to break in cold into the European market after the War, it would have cost us $10,000,000. The Peace Ship cost $\frac{1}{20}$ of that and made Ford a household word all over the continent." In 1922, when a magazine writer was to appeal to Ford to mediate the dispute between Turkey and Britain, Ford retorted that another European war was inevitable, and "the U.S. should get into it at the beginning and clean them all up."

But Ford was never a man to admit failure. At worst, he kept quiet about the adventure afterwards. Sorensen relates of Ford's homecoming that he had not a word to say about the Expedition, and Sorensen never heard him say one in the years that followed.

His remark that he did not regret the Peace Ship, and learned more from it than from any of his undertakings, may have an ambiguous ring. Yet the same ability to see gain in defeat may be observed in his comment on the failure of prohibition. "At least it made a lot of people clean up their cellars." Possibly his belief in the doctrine of reincarnation preserved him from viewing discouragements with finality.

In his World War II article in *Scribner's Commentator*, "An American Foreign Policy," Ford, now that he found use for it, went into detail about what he felt he had "learned" on the Peace Ship. "A ghastly trade was carried on behind the lines. Raw materials produced in France and England were shipped to Germany to be converted into munitions; likewise German goods moved into France for processing into war machinery to kill and maim the very people who produced them."

Certainly in his telegram to this writer on the occasion of the Expedition's twenty-fifth anniversary, he strikes a clear note: "At least we did not diminish the life and love that were in the world."

Even Sorensen did not take an altogether negative view of the venture. He wrote: "All in all, Mr. and Mrs. Ford did not come out too badly in the long run. The cry was that this was a war to end all wars. Eternal peace was the purpose. Did we get it?"

12

Still in the Trenches at Christmas

"Expert advisor" Rosika Schwimmer had gone on ahead of the peace brigade to try to soften up Denmark for her party. But although she strove to display as homey a personality as a crock of cookies in a pantry, Frau Schwimmer did not succeed in mellowing the Minister of Justice. The Minister's aide routed her out of bed on her first morning in Copenhagen to officially inform her that the ordinance prohibiting public meetings and speeches, in the interests of Danish neutrality, would be fully enforced against the Ford Expedition.

Thus the third week of the peace delegates' stay in Europe did not open with brightening aspects for achievement.

Yet, as things worked out in practice, the peace party got around the law very nicely. In fact, the Danish sojourn was declared more successful than that in Sweden. There was more scope for person-to-person confrontations. The delegates got to meet and talk with more people on an individual basis than elsewhere. All this was because the meetings were arranged under "private" auspices, which circumvented the ordinance. As long as assemblages were technically private, admitting guests by invitation only, there could be no official objection.

All kinds of diversified groups, well set up for conducting meetings in this fashion—socialists, liberals, Single-Taxers, young organizations, peace societies, students' fraternities, even the influential liberal paper *Politiken,* all vied with one another in the arrangement of meetings. Since there was a good deal of competition in this matter of doing well by the Expedition, invitations and publicity were profusely distributed, and the leaders and members of the various groups worked overtime to make their events a success.

Besides formal functions, presided over by a Thorwaldsen-like blond and vital leader, Olaf Forchhammer of the Danish Committee, there were sightseeing excursions arranged for the pilgrims, with a Danish partner assigned to each so that there was the maximum chance for direct contact. The Americans got to see such points of interest as the ornate new City Hall, the Olyptothek, Tivoli gardens and the Rosenberg castle. Nearly everyone made it a point to visit Elsinore and the legendary castle which the Danes call Kronberg Castle and where Shakespeare placed his mad prince *Amleth.*

And the communication was not limited to the man-in-the-street. It was the first time the Expedition had occasion to come into close contact with the social upper crust. One of the first large meetings took place in the palatial mansion of the great art patron and collector, Vagn Jacobsen. Since he was quite a social style-setter, attendance at this event by all the bluebloods became *de rigueur.* The noted author Sven Lange expressed the general tenor of the reception when he said, "Every thinking and feeling person in this country respects and sympathizes with the strong will which has carried the expedition through and with the idea it embodies."

Lending a note of real quality, in the realm of music, to these festivities, was a Vikinglike operatic tenor, who specialized in Wagnerian roles at the Royal Danish Opera House. This blond youth of noble height, head, and vocal range had attached himself firmly to the Ford party, with its American connotations of opportunity and promise. The possessor of the golden voice with the affinity for the gold-plated Expedition serenaded the pilgrims with their national anthem, with *arie* and *liede*. He went by the name of Lauritz Melchior.

Another signal event in Copenhagen was a reception in *Politiken* Hall, to which both the "grand old men" and the *avant garde* of the literati and the Danish art world came. "The peace pilgrims have won all Danish hearts," said the editor of *Politiken*, and this was picked up and carried by the whole Scandinavian press.

There was even word from the long-silent absent leader, Ford himself. He wired that he was feeling better.

While in Copenhagen, a Russian newsman visited the Expedition with a collection of more than 500 clippings on the peace pilgrimage, culled from the Russian press, both in Moscow and St. Petersburg and in the provinces. Thus the delegates could plume themselves with having added a spark to the conflagration soon to sweep out Czarism.

It was also in Copenhagen that the Expedition lost one of its delegates—the glamorous Inez Mulholland had already quit the scene in a huff and gone home to her husband, the very social Mr. Boissevain. Now the redoubtable S.S. McClure, who had been dubbed the "Naughty Boy Sam" of the party, and who had presented the spectacle of a man wrestling with his own soul in full view of everybody since the preparedness battle on the Oscar, made the schism official by deserting the "anti-preparedness" pilgrims.

"I am not offended," he explained, pleasantly, to which his comrades-against-arms might have responded as one, "But *we* are!" It was reported that he was en route to Berlin.

A drenching downpour shrouded the station at Copenhagen as the delegation entrained on its most spectacular trip— through Germany—to The Hague, but outstanding Danish pacifists gathered to see them off, nonetheless.

Ford behielt Recht.

This final leg of the pilgrimage, to carry the pacifists across belligerent soil, represented the greatest problem encountered yet.

No neutral vessel big enough to accommodate the delegation would risk the mine and submarine-infested waters of the North Sea at less than $50,000 worth of insurance, and although the much-enduring Gaston Plantiff took provisional option on a ship under these conditions, negotiations proceeded to get "necessary transit" permission to cross Germany. Here some "unofficial" business was undertaken between the Expedition's Dr. Egan and his friend the German minister, Count Brockdorff-Rantzau. The result was the granting of transit-permission from the Imperial Government in Berlin, under circumstances which, in those days, aroused only admiration in the pilgrims for the efficiency of the transportation technique. Twenty years afterward, in the period of the Hitler genocide program, this means of shipping human beings would have carried quite another connotation. The pacifists were told that their transit permission did not include the right to touch German soil; therefore, they were to be expressed through the Fatherland on a sealed train.

Plenty of German instructions had to be complied with, and it was almost more of a production to get the delegates in shape for the sealed train-ride than for the Oscar voyage. Every scrap of writing, even picture postcards, was *verboten*. The delegates were warned that all coin would be confiscated, so conversion to paper currency was essential, and pictures, cameras, opera glasses, even personal letters either had to be sent home to the States or mailed to Holland.

Finally, after an almost night-long check of visas with the German consul, the Americans were ferried over from Denmark to the German port of Warnemuende, having been once serenaded in farewell. The train into which they were to be "sealed" for the no-stop transit through Germany—the first tourists to cross, or even to enter Germany since the outbreak of the war—provided by the military authorities, stood awaiting them on the dock, surrounded by soldiers.

The peace pilgrims stood on the platform in the dusk in a drizzling rain as their names were called from the list and they were permitted, one at a time, to board the train.

But even once locked inside the train, of which each car was also locked, the pacifists noted plenty of evidences of the war. Posted notices advised that, when the train was passing over bridges or under tunnels, the windows and doors should be locked, because spies had on occasion thrown bombs with the aim of blowing up the railroad. Other signs called on the public to eat sparingly and not waste food. One listed ten rules, among them, not to pare potatoes before cooking, to save breadcrumbs, and abstain from meat.

Dining accommodations for the 200 passengers consisted of one dining car. It was explained that dining cars were being used to transport the wounded. The pilgrims found little to complain of in the food, although there was no meat, something of a comedown from the menu of the Grand Hotel. Dinner was vegetable soup, fish omelet and vegetables, bread and butter, cheese and beer. The gray color of the bread surprised the delegates, but they could not criticize its flavor.

From the food to the attitude of the soldiers, the pacifists decided that if you had to have war, the Germans knew how to run one. The sealed train ran on time, a factor particularly impressive to its American passengers. Military security was underplayed, and the officers were quite relaxed, almost convivial. William C. Bullitt remarked that apparently a yachting party with a few revolvers could have taken Warnemuende, and he admired the fact that the place had been painted up. Through the windows of the houses, as they passed through Hamburg, picturesque vignettes of family life—even if the head of the family was absent—gratified the delegates. The station platforms were well-swept, and no armed guards were posted. One railroad employee in a long military coat and cap was a fragile young woman.

Efforts of the pacifists to pick up information were fruitless. Little of note could be observed in connection with the war except trainload after trainload of ammunition which seemed to pass all night. At a stop at a Red Cross relief station we saw about fifty wounded German soldiers. The throngs that gathered to watch the train pass gazed impassively, with the exception of one lieutenant who raised his helmet in salute to the peace pilgrims. The spiritless faces and haunted eyes of German travelers in passing trains impressed the delegates who read in them "a plea for peace." A large sign at the head of each station platform read: *Soldiers, beware how you talk in the presence of strangers: they may be spies.*

A special guard of troopers on the train showed the peace

contingent punctilious courtesy, while standing watch that the regulations attending the transit permission were maintained. This smoothness with which the Germans handled everything went over very big with the Americans. One correspondent, John W. English of the *Boston Traveler*, waxed almost rhapsodic in contemplation of the German flair of doing things right.

> If the world had a little more of that efficiency it would be a good thing . . . One of the things which impressed us most in going through Germany was the feeling of security which all pilgrims had when they were in the hands of the Germans. They felt that they were going to be properly taken care of because they realized the Germans knew how to do things right. That's what it means to have a reputation for efficiency. I had that feeling, and when I began to ask questions, I found that nearly every one of the party shared the feeling.

This American affinity for German know-how was unmarred by any perception of the "Prussianization" which Owen Wister's impassioned diatribe had deplored. On the contrary, the peace pilgrims were seeing something of the old idealized, *gemutliche* German tradition. In fact, one German lieutenant who boarded the train at Hamburg, notwithstanding the Iron Cross on his coat, unbent enough with the pilgrims to felicitate them on their mission. "No man has more faith in this Expedition than I," he told them. "It is bound to shorten the war because of the psychological effect it will have."

It was two-thirty in the morning when the tired peace crew pulled into Bentheim, the last station in Germany. The Americans whiled away their wait in the gloomy station dozing on the window sills, their luggage, or the few chairs, or trying to keep awake over "coffee" or relaxing with a beer at the restaurant. The guards here, posted twenty feet apart, were taciturn, and the pilgrims could get no response out of them.

The Americans were waiting to be searched, but then the

word came, after a token search of about a dozen pieces of hand luggage, that since they had adhered to the letter of the instructions, they would not be subjected to this. There in the somber railroad station, at four o'clock in the morning, the pilgrims let out a cheer for their "belligerent" hosts.

In the eerily-lit railway restaurant, Dr. Jones, sensing another psychological moment for a speech, delivered one of thanks, and three cheers were given the German lieutenant who had extended the courtesies. The lieutenant replied in kind, wishing the pilgrims success in their purpose and a happy journey.

A German officer examining passports asked one of the correspondents, "When is peace coming, and where is it?"

"Peace is in the air!" said the American.

"Well, you're angels then," said the German officer.

The "angels" boarded the Dutch train and pulled into their final destination, The Hague, at noon on January 8. Here the high level of hospitality sustained throughout the party's three-weeks' whirlwind through the neutral capitals was manifested by a welcoming committee, including a representative of the Dutch Parliament and the usual bevy of attractive girls, and a gracious welcome to the accommodations at the Hotel Wittenburg.

The correspondents, however, immediately met with a decided shock. It had been a strenuous tour in Scandinavia and a sleepless night on the sealed train, and we newsmen felt a particular need of an appropriate libation in our wearied state.

Profound was the consternation, then, when we found that our rooms were reserved in a vegetarian-temperance hotel. This had been the dirty-work of a pacifist-delegate whom Mme. Schwimmer had entrusted with the hotel arrangements. The story was that The Hague was so crowded with German and Belgian refugees that this was the only recourse, but some of the reporters were never sure. We, perpetrators of so many jokes on the Expedition, found the last laugh was on us, and where it hurt the most, at that.

"I'm a sick man!" the protests went up at the dry hotel. It was no use. "We'll send out for a bottle," we quickly reassured ourselves, in our first alarm, only to find that the manager courteously and inexorably relieved us of any long-necked parcels. No "stuff" went upstairs. It might have been easier to have taken the hostesses to their rooms, had we felt up to it, in our parched state.

We strove to fortify ourselves in the dining room, and were confronted with health foods and vegetarian cutlets compounded of cereal and ground nuts. We might as well have been back on the German train. In despair, one newsman tipped back his chair, took out a cigarette and lit up. "No smoking, sir!" said the manager.

While the correspondents, bereft of stimulants and steak, languished, the pacifists flourished. Holland was of more negotiable size than their earlier host-nations, and by one demonstration apiece in Amsterdam and Rotterdam and two in The Hague, the mission was able to reach more people. Also, the Dutch were generally bilingual, and the interruptions of running translations could be dispensed with. Besides this, the Expedition had gotten a shot in the arm by the addition of Norwegian, Swedish and Danish delegates, so that it had now an authentically international quality.

Press reaction was divided, as in Norway, but at least the Dutch, pro or con, took the undertaking seriously. One major paper, the *Nieuwe Rooterdamsche Courant*, hailed the Expedition: It comes, like most other foreigners who have visited this country in the last year, on "business." But its "business" is of a highly idealistic character . . . all it is striving after is to serve humanity by bringing it peace.

. . . it is even probable that peace will reach Europe along another road than that traveled by the Ford party.

Let us nonetheless recognize the fine thought which in-
spires the party . . . It sees only a warring, a bewildered
Europe; armies of millions destroying each other like mad-
men; the coming ruin of the entire old European world.
And it desires, urged by a similar love for all, to bring back
to all at least a small portion of happiness. Is that silly or
wrong?

"It will not succeed." What does that matter? Ford's Expedition may bring about no great deed; it represents a
great conception, and that is truly some reason in these
times for extending it a special welcome.

At The Hague, it was not the enemy without, but the enemy
within that rose rampant. The Expedition was "a typical American community" to the bitter, bitter end. It was election time
for the delegates, and with the mudslinging and charges of
"fix!" it was just like home.

The "war in mid-ocean" between the "preparedness" and
"anti-preparedness" factions on the Oscar II had indeed been
merely a good, vigorous, healthy airing of views,—a whole-
some democratic discussion—compared to the battle royal that
broke out in the historic peace-city of The Hague when the
pacifists hit town.

But even before the pacifists, who, after all, like Caesar,
were ambitious, came to lock horns, there was trouble with the
local peace people.

Pacifism was not, as we have seen, necessarily an indigenously American virtue—or vice—even though Ford's own brand
may have come close to it. In fact, every country formed their
own peace groups, and Holland enjoyed considerable primacy
in the field with her own *Nederlandsche Anti-Oorlog Raad.*

Thus, from the very outset of the Netherlands sojourn, the
home-grown pacifists and the Ford party began to step on each
others' toes. First off, the Raad invited, of all representatives of
the Ford group, some of the journalists—still disgruntled and
thirsty—to a small reception at which to free their minds on

CESSATION OF HOSTILITIES

THE HAGUE

NELSON HARDING, BROOKLYN EAGLE.

the subject of their Ford competitors.

This was to touch off the battle of the "maximists" and the "minimists," an international controversy after the merely domestic squabble of the "preparedness" and "anti-preparedness" people. Dr. Dresselhuijs explained that the Raad's "minimum" program had been evolved at The Hague conference the previous April, in contrast to the Ford "maximum" or all-out program, which the Raad deemed impracticable.

As for the Dutch people, the Ford Expedition never made a ripple. Peace pilgrims were old stuff to them. Holland had at the moment no less than fifty-seven different peace groups functioning, and new ones broke upon the scene continually, so that one more or less was of no consequence to the man in the street—or on the canal. What did throw the Dutch considerably, however, was that the Ford people should fail to follow the "Take me to your leader" approach, since in the midst of motley peace groups, peace "party line" was set by the Raad, to which, in fact, every fourth male in Holland belonged.

As a matter of fact, the Raad had only just presented its own appeal to the Netherlands Parliament to take initiative in the very question of a neutral conference. (The Parliament, like all the other neutral governments, was reported "waiting for the psychological moment"—that moment everybody awaited which never came.)

While the Ford peace competitors rode roughshod over the pacifist "Establishment," a committee of Dutch women, showing either feminine tact or latent national feeling, took care to invite the Raad to send delegates to the Neutral Conference for Continual Mediation. While this matter hung fire, the goings-on with the Americans in the name of peace, according to one correspondent, made war seem almost preferable.

Sworn to "forget all selfishness and leave personal ambition out of the great work that was to be done," the pacifists still seemed to feel free to carry on a spot of electioneering, if not hanky-panky, and rumors of under-the-table deals for the election of permanent delegates threw everybody into a turmoil. While the fur flew, Dr. Charles Aked, in a huff, withdrew the resolution of "War and Peace" framed by himself together with Lochner and the Tennessee newspaper editor, George F. Milton. This resolution had offered a slate from which the American delegates should be chosen.

Aked declared that there was suspicion that he was nominating himself, which was perfectly true—in fact, an understatement. The belief among other delegates was that Aked, imbued with the cloak-and-dagger atmosphere of the Scandinavian hotels, had closed the deal with Plantiff as far back as Copenhagen: he got the job, in consideration of the payment of all his expenses, his wife's fare to Europe, her living expenses, and the "honorarium" of $15,000 for the first six months or less of the conference, and of $10,000 for the rest of the year, if it went on that long; while the other delegates would get $5,000 for the first three months and less thereafter.

Since it was a foregone conclusion that Henry Ford, Jane Addams, and William Jennings Bryan would serve, this actually left only one American delegate to be elected.

Upon Aked's withdrawal of the resolution, Harry C. Evans, another editor—of the *Des Moines Yeoman Shield,*—entered a proposal of his own empowering Plantiff, Lochner, and Mrs. William Bross Light, a Texas-born Smith girl, former math teacher, wife of the millionaire socialist, and cohort of Rosika Schwimmer and Jane Addams, to appoint the five American delegates and alternates.

"To vote for this resolution would be to make the supreme blunder of our lives!" shouted John Barry, leaping to his feet. He declared that it was asking them virtually to disfranchise themselves by entrusting full power to a few who did not have at heart the same interests as the entire delegation as a body. "If the press finds out that the delegation as a whole had no voice in the choosing of the delegates, we shall all be put to ridicule!" he added (as if this would be a new experience).

Mrs. May Wright Sewall, that *grande dame* of women's organizations from Indianapolis, observed that the big mistake they were making was to assume that the Expedition was to function democratically. She said that it wasn't working that way and had never been meant to. "It was nothing but a great big house party," she said. "The most historic house party that ever took place." The delegates laughed.

"Are we ready to vote on the resolution?" asked Dr. Jenkin Lloyd Jones, chairman of the session.

"This whole scheme is a frame-up!" shouted Barry, on his feet again. "Put this thing through and there'll be misery and disaster for the whole undertaking."

"Sit down! Sit him down!" shouted the delegates.

"Mr. Chairman, I protest the use of the word frame-up," said Dr. Aked.

But there was no stopping Barry now, much less getting him
to retract anything. He plunged furiously on. "On the Oscar II
when we were in mid-ocean, we were suddenly asked to sign a
platform in criticism of President Wilson's program of national
defense, and told that those of us who did not sign would not
have a final voice in choosing the permanent delegates for the
neutral conference. That seemed to indicate that we were to be
allowed to vote in the final selection of those delegates. It
would be nothing but a scandal and frame-up to vote for a
resolution as autocratic and unAmerican as this!"

"No! No!" roared the protest. Dr. Jones' voice, again asking if
the delegates were ready for a vote, was drowned out in the
melee. "A skirmish," one delegate called it; it was peace pande-
monium.

This was one brawl too many for Plantiff. Normally, the
Ford man tried to "run a happy ship," but on this occasion he
had stiff words for the guests, the import of which would be
too devastating for them to take seriously, since he held the
purse strings. He said he didn't want to serve on any committee. He was through with committees. He wanted to get back
to his desk where he could get something real done, and where
there was a little sanity. He said he could wish, as Mr. Ford's
representative, that such procedure might be followed as Mr.
Ford would approve.

Accordingly, the resolution was voted down, and Ford,
Bryan, and Miss Addams were elected by proclamation. The
remaining two unchosen and the five alternates had to come
from the delegates on the floor.

So they were all back to where they started. Parliamentary
procedure went to pot. All may well have been quiet on the
Western front compared with the shape of things at the peace
meeting in The Hague.

It took an hour and a half simply to calm the delegates down
enough to record a voice election, a farcical one enough if you
were a stickler for the Marquis of Queensberry procedures.

Senator Helen Ring Robinson of Colorado, noted for being able to beat up a cake as well as a political opponent, thus maintaining her femininity as ferociously as her feminism, got up out of a sickbed, to which she had been confined in serious condition, and came down to withdraw her name from the slate.

"I have watched this election of yours with keen interest," she addressed the delegates, "to observe how an organization which has come to Europe on a high and holy mission conducts its election. And I have seen your padded election lists. I have observed the methods of your executive committee, methods plainly copied from the Tammany Halls of corrupt American politics. Very simply and sincerely and sadly I tell you that your election is tainted, and every delegate and alternate chosen by such methods is tainted, too.

"Under such circumstances I cannot allow my name to remain on the ticket since, although I have lost much time and money and strength and health on this trip, I have kept my self-respect.

"I may add that I retain some sense of humor, too, so I can smile lightly at the zeal of my withdrawal, since I have the honor of knowing that, under present conditions, I could not be elected."

"Senator," the chairman, Dr. Jones, felicitated her before she withdrew, "every word you say is the truth, and I agree with you."

Judge Lindsey, who up till then had taken no part in the whole fracas, asked just before the ballots were cast, that his own name not be entered. He declined to state a reason, but said that he had "a very good one."

Yet after all the furor died down, and when, after many ballots had been taken, the election results were made known, it seemed as if, as in so many larger elections, a basic good sense had prevailed in the end. Even the cynical newsmen, raw-nerved from involuntary abstemiousness, had to concede that the choice of Mrs. Joseph Fels, the German-born proponent of good Judeo-Christian relations, social justice, and a religious interpretation of man's relationship to the soil and to God's law, and of Dr. Charles Aked, were the best available.

Runners-up had been Professor George W. Kirchwey, Professor Woolsey of Yale, and Rabbi Stephen S. Wise, whose reply to Ford's invitation had been hardly that of a bona fide pacifist:

> Though I abhor war I should deem it the deepest spiritual calamity of centuries if any peace were effected that did not redeem Belgium from the wrong inflicted upon it by its invaders, that did not make noble France outwardly whole again, that did not deal a final and crushing blow to the militarism of the last forty years which Prussia did most to foster.

Also named had been Emily Balch, but the absence of these four made it impossible to know their stand on disarmament, clarification of which would have been imperative to render them eligible as delegates.

At the next day's session the pro tem delegates were elected. This was not accomplished without some revival of dissension, and it took six ballots to elect the alternates, Emily Balch, Professor Kirchwey, Judge Lindsey, Dr. Jenkin Lloyd Jones and John D. Barry. The latter was known not to be one hundred per cent behind disarmament, and a further split occurred, with Barry finally defeating Peabody by one vote. All these elections, however, were to be subject to Henry Ford's approval.

There remained another knotty question for the peacers to scrap about. They had established the "who," but what about the "where?" Now they were divided into the Stockholmers and the Haguers. The Scandinavian delegates, as well as those Americans with palmy memories of the Grand Hotel, where they had lived it up in a manner to which pacifists were never accustomed, naturally favored Stockholm. The women who had been at the Women's International Peace Conference the year before just as naturally preferred their old stomping ground, The Hague.

Dr. Jenkin Lloyd Jones delivered himself of his own views on the geographical problem: "Should we hold our conference in The Hague it would appear only as a diminuendo movement, and would not command sufficient attention, whereas, if it were held in Stockholm our success would be assured, for there we were greeted with organized enthusiasm, and received with open arms."

Here Plantiff spoke up and asked that Henry Ford be accorded at least one privilege, that of determining where he should go on keeping them all; and he asked that the vote taken be merely preferential. Stockholm was voted. Influential had been their old friend Mayor Lindhagen's appeal that the peace idea be provided as many peace centers as possible, and with The Hague and Switzerland already established as such, that a third, in the north, be erected between Germany and Russia.

It would seem that this left not even the Peace delegates anything to fight over; but there was still the burning issue of disarmament, sparked all over again by the wording of a Scandinavian resolution calling for "abolition of armaments."

So it was John Barry once more to the fore, warning the delegates not to commit their "most serious blunder," and demanding the substitution of "limitation" for "abolition."

"No! No! Sit down! Militarist!"

The vicious circle was completed on the very day that the Expedition was to sail home on the Rotterdam. It was a hung peace party. The other American delegates were for complete disarmament and they'd fight anybody who was for limitation.

As the Expedition broke up, it left two neutral nations embattled and an ultimatum hanging fire.

In the end, it was a case of "you can't fight city hall," with the Dutch delegates unable to vote on anything, because they still hadn't gotten the green light from the Anti-Oorlog Raad. The Scandinavians were homesick and worn out from the private war the pacifists had put on in doing the spadework for settling the World War, and issued an ultimatum to the Dutch —twenty-four hours to elect their delegates and vote on the final resolution.

Having pitted two neutrals against each other, the rest of the pacifists cut for home, or, in some cases, petitioned for a rest cure from peace in the snowy Alps or sunny Spain. Others, with newborn interest in organized war, wanted to take a look at battle fronts, Western or Eastern.

Those younger newspaper reporters who had not tired living out of their steamer trunks—no one traveled without one then —were eager to get to the Western front, where the curtain was going up on the third year of the struggle and massive drives were in preparation—Verdun, the Somme, Jutland. But alas, Allied regulations forbade any journalist from entering France from anywhere except an Allied country. A number of us took the long and somewhat perilous ride back to the U.S., only to recross the Atlantic to France and the fighting fronts.

Those of us who were invited by the German General Staff —propaganda section—to junket down to the Rumanian-Transylvanian front to take a look at von Mackensen's victorious operations, were permitted to detach from the Ford Expedition, provided we rejoined the S.S. Rotterdam in Holland for the homeward voyage. The passage home would be forefeited if the passenger failed to show up. Plantiff had now pulled the purse strings shut and this was his ruling. The "house party" was over. The guests were on their own. Anybody who couldn't manage independently, if he didn't have any more business in Europe, could go home.

One prominent European asked, "What business did they have there in the first place?"

13

The Sneer Heard Round the World

A judicial, if not judicious, ruling on the Henry Ford Peace Expedition was handed down in a New York City court when a cab driver who had gotten a summons for a violation pleaded that "the Ford people" had told him he could operate his taxi as an owner without a chauffeur's license.

Whereas Magistrate Murphy ruled, "The Ford people are all in Europe, and they are crazy."

In the British House of Commons' share in the world-wide sanity hearing on the Peace Expedition, it was asked, "If they have the right of asylum here, can we certify them to be insane?"

A marine engineer remarked, "It's a good thing the Oscar had two screws. Ford apparently has one loose."

One Broadway first-nighter believed Ford was crazy like a fox. "Peace will have to come some time and if it comes inside of two years, then this fellow will be able to take the credit for it."

One of the more literate of the many journalist chroniclers of the Expedition likened it to *The Hunting of the Snark, An*

Agony in Eight Fits, Lewis Carroll's long nonsense-ballad, in which

> The crew was complete: it included a Boots,
>   A Maker of Bonnets and Hoods,
> A Barrister brought to arrange their disputes,
>   And a Broker, to value their goods,

and, in the pursuit of the evanescent *Snark,* was menaced by jubjubs and boojums, although well-armed with thimbles, forks, hope, and soap, and fraught with miscalculations:

> He had forty-two boxes, all carefully packed,
>   With his name clearly painted on each:
> But, since he omitted to mention the fact,
>   They were all left behind on the beach.

According to the refrain of a Fordian's acrostic, more serious-minded if less metrical,

> I know it is a peace ship,
> And I really think, don't you
> That long before we reach the shore
> 'Twill be a *friendship* too.

However, press coverage denoted very much otherwise. The headlines ran "Ford Peace Ship Called Hate Ship," "Peace Delegates Return Still in Excellent Voice," "Cherubim and Seraphim Banged Each Other with Peace Harps," and "Ford Pilgrims Near New York Full of Fight."

The embarkation at Hoboken, which had been saluted by a *Mutt and Jeff* comic strip depicting the delegates required to check their weapons at the dock, and representations of Henry Ford addressing the swordfish, "Peace-fish, sheath your swords!" while inquiring, "is my tail-light on?," had signalled no achievement during the six weeks' Expedition to change the tenor of its press.

"It's rather unusual," had been the Rev. Caroline B. Crane's comment, befitting in dry elegance a female of the cloth. The

LIFE ON THE ARK OF PEACE

By T. E. Powers, the Famous Cartoonist

T. E. POWERS, THE STAR COMPANY.

Evening Mail's Sara Moore predicted, "It may be that we shall only furnish the gentle reader with a few pathetic smiles—literally at Mr. Ford's expense."

"Dr. Pease Didn't Go Because of Mother," one headline apologized for anti-tobacconist Charles Giffin Pease. The cartoon "The Flivver at Sea" designated the delegates as "lady cranks," "plain cranks," and "rah-rah boys," as the stacks shot "hot air" and "soothing syrup," while in the somewhat free-wheeling imagery of the official song of the Ford Peace Mission, this clouded-crystal-ball prognostication was offered:

The cannibal, Zulu and Indian Chief
The army and the navy will also come to grief
The warriors of old lived with murder in their hearts
The military spirit will be one of the lost arts.

As the delegates gave out with their "Peace and Prosperity" chorus all over Europe: "*We love the dear old Stars and Stripes, because we are Ameri-can,*" the papers reported the flesh-and-blood enactment of the pursuit of the Snark under heads like "Ford's Floating Trench," "Where Are We At? Ford Party's Cry," "More of the Peace That Passeth All Understanding," "Pilgrims Hold First Meeting at Zoo," "Says Pacifists Coo, But Like to Fight," "Ford Trip Running Fight," and "Flivver, Big Ford Show, Ends in Dutch Burlesque."

Meanwhile, a theatrical burlesque of the Expedition was presented by the Crescent Athletic Club at the Academy of Music in Brooklyn, featuring John F. Kelly in the role of "Mme. Swimmer," in a rousing finale, "When I get Back to the U.S.A."

The delegates arriving back in the U.S.A. had their private interpretations, which were duly offered up in the public post-mortem. "Too many ministers and crabs on the peace ship," was the Rev. Dr. Jenkin Lloyd Jones' diagnosis. "Too much joy ride and women's talk," F. Munroe Smock, the representative of the Governor of Idaho, was quoted as analyzing what there was too much of. As to what the undertaking lacked, "*Moses was needed!*" one delegate summed it up. Failure had been freely acknowledged earlier by the delegates themselves. "We are in an awful hole," Aked admitted. "The game is up," Lindsey said.

The ship that was "launched upon one vast wave of ridicule" has been memorialized by a Russian writer in apprehension of a new war. "They (the people of the world) are again on the verge of a fit of madness that will lead to bloodshed and destruction. The moment is near when they will once more grab each other by the throat, start on another brawl—and succeed

THE FLIVVER AT SEA.

this time in finally destroying the culture and economy of the
world . . ." He also mentions a program for shelters "comfortably appointed and electrically lighted and heated throughout."

The writer was Maxim Gorki, the year 1925, one hardly remembered as much for madness nor even for vergence upon it

as others since. Gorki calls the Expedition "the hopeless whim of a wise maniac." In the terrible days of the accursed war, he wrote: "Ford was among the first to speak out on Peace, in language noble and inspiring. But at the end . . . he started to prepare munitions for the extermination of mankind."

A more restrained personality, Vermont pacifist Sarah Cleghorn, epitomized by Robert Frost as a poet and a saint, prefers understatement: "that effort to save the lives of young men which aroused mirth among some people."

The delegation of students, too, were not reticent about their own occasion for youthful rancor, directed mainly at their chaperone, the high-minded New-England-born Mrs. Ada Morse ("Policeman") Clark. To her scornful question, "How can you dance while Europe lies bleeding?" the students' attitude was that since symbolically sharing the travails of Europe wasn't going to staunch her wounds, they might as well dance.

No greater felicity between their elders was reflected in the report of the final Hague dispute—"In the ensuing wrangle several women burst into tears," nor in its depiction of lady pacifists battering each other over the head with their parasols, while Gaston Plantiff crawled rapidly for an exit on his hands and knees in between their skirts. Another *Mutt and Jeff* strip showed Jeff, in uniform deserting at top speed, and coming face to face with Mutt, who has deserted already.

> Jeff: "Back to the front!"
>   What's in the rear?"
> Mutt: "The Ford Peace Party. Hey—
>   wait a minute! Where are you going?"
> Jeff: "Back to the front!"

And in stanzas not altogether unworthy of Carroll himself, one bard celebrated the internecine battling thus:

> "Can the scrap," said Mme. Schwimmer,
> "It is too much to endure."

"Let me have one smash at *Hanna*,"
Pleaded S. McClure.

This couplet commemorates purely symbolically "the War in Mid-Ocean," inasmuch as McClure and Governor Hanna had been on the same side.

All this time, it was peace-business as usual for the dedicated Louis Lochner. The young professional pacifist was inured to public ridicule, so much so that any sympathetic encounter became a glorious occasion to him, although it could portend no practical advantage. But herein lay a deep difference among the variegated membership of the Expedition. The all-American success-motive which inspired the rank-and-file Fordites and Ford himself to accomplish something definite was absent to the traditional pacifists, who functioned on a more abstract plane. In reporting the identical event, one correspondent counted "a handful" of people, where Louis Lochner saw "throngs." Neither lied. The orthodox pacifists lived in a continous beatific vision. But those followers, who took seriously even the pragmatic spirit of the "out-of-the-trenches-by-Christmas" slogan, were inevitably disappointed.

And while they were singing "After the Ball is Over," Lochner pursued the chimera—or the snark—almost as if he hadn't noticed that everybody had gone home—in fact, as if now that they were gone, he could settle down to a little serious peace-work. To get the delegates from Switzerland, which, like Holland, suffered from a saturation of peace people, necessitated a personal trip by Lochner. While in Switzerland, he was "thrilled" by the sympathy of the great art critic, musician and author, Romain Rolland. On the return trip through Germany, the peace people found they had worn out their welcome, and were put on the German blacklist!

In Stockholm the conference met daily at the still agent-infested Grand Hotel, but now in a no-nonsense atmosphere of committees, multi-linguistics and drafts of appeals. Two appeals, one to the neutrals and one to the belligerents, were produced, and if the delegates seemed ever sublimely confident, possibly it was in a certain dim clairvoyance, for the letter and spirit of these "Appeals" are matters of common acceptance to believers in the present-day United Nations.

But the party was all over for those who came home, many in high dudgeon, such as chief stenographer Rexford L. Holmes, who brought suit against the Expedition for libel. He had been accused of embezzling $5,000. Many other claims were filed, such as that of a teacher never reimbursed for $1,500 advanced by herself to secure a substitute for her professorial chair while she sat as a delegate at Stockholm.

Uniform disorder had characterized the Expedition from its leavetaking to its return. Even one bit of human—or canine—interest to the homecoming, misfired. The North Dakota editor, Sam H. Clark, owned a faithful dog who couldn't wait to greet his master. Accordingly, the dog came East and occupied reservations (presumably made for him) at the Hotel Majestic, where he was cared for by the staff until Clark docked. When the ship came in, the dog took a cab (with a bellboy) to the pier. En route, the taxi door flew open, and the over-eager dog sprang out and tore off down Fifth Avenue. Sam Clark was met by the chagrined bellhop. The dog was ultimately discovered through his disconsolate howls in Greeley Square. It seemed as if nobody could get together, not even a man and his dog.

If the guardians of the Ford image—the Liebolds, the Plantiffs and the strong-arm squads—had any notions that when the curtain dropped on the last act of this odd odyssey, the whole screwball episode would vanish and be forgotten like last Sunday's supplement, they were very quickly disillusioned. Certainly there were many bitter and serious calumniators who despised Henry Ford. They kept up a barrage of vitriolic criticism lasting through the months, even years. To this brand of abuse, some of it palpably libelous, the Ford courtiers were by this time pretty much inured. What hurt was the sarcasm, the lampooning. Here the ex-correspondents who came back from the junket were effective and persistent.

When the reporters decided to reactivate the shipboard fraternity of Friendly and Vacillating Sons of Saint Vitus, they got together at a dinner at Keen's Chop House, off Herald Square in New York. Such newspaper stalwarts as the *N.Y. World's* Joseph Jefferson O'Neill, elegant and aloof with his fedora and ivory-handled cane, and the abstemious Rhodes scholar, Elmer Davis of the *N.Y. Times*, elected "Egregious Epileptor," and Philadelphia's very rich embryo diplomat, Bill Bullitt, joined eighteen or twenty fellow correspondents in a "class reunion" which was a classic of ribald sneering and good-natured reviling.

For the occasion the boys published a satirical four-page tabloid news-sheet they call *The Scandihoovian Clarion*. It was printed on, of all places, the presses of the old *N.Y. Herald* which were visible through huge plate glass windows set below the sidewalk on Herald Square, opposite Macy's.

The Clarion featured such departments as: *JNEWS–JOTTINGS*, the spelling an influence, no doubt, of the contact with the Dutch press. There was an *ADJVERTISING* section carrying a number of display ads including one advertising the *HJOTEL NATIONALE*, "The House of a Thousand Scandals Right in the Center of Everything, with Police Protection and Baths for Persons Contemplating Crossing the German Border." Also advertised was "The Little Hungry—Eat there and Die Happy," and the vaudeville show "Fording the Fjords," in five obscenes, listed as these:

I. The Horsecar the Second, North Atlantic Crosstown.
II. In Hale Norway.
III. Sunny Sweden.
IV. Formal Denmark, or Ten Nights in a Bare Room.
V. Hague and Haig, or the Lingerie Cafe.

There were other ads of biting sarcasm such as the one levelled at the much harassed Gaston, the paymaster:

Bargain Sale:
This week at Gas Plantiff's Place; one set of shop-worn "papers"—also some old peace programs slightly soiled. Several bunches of receipts. Highest bid takes all.

And the one slanted at Mme. Schwimmer:

Wanted agents: no investment required. Use your Powers of Conversation. Sell peace to wealthy pacifists. Interest the old and young. Easy way to fortune. Territory unlimited.

A "news" story, headlined "Peace At All Prices Reigns at a Low Market in Stockholm," discussed the "Unofficial Conference's" search for "Why is Europe?"

"Louis P. Lochner, when interviewed by the native correspondents exclusively this morning is reported to have replied in his native tongue, 'Smush!' Stocks rose and bowed politely at this prediction." This item concluded that there was confidence in high official circles that in ten years' time the conferees, if not able to answer the main question, might at least be able to ask "Why is Austria-Hungary?"

The Executive Session of the Friendly and Vacillating Sons of Saint Vitus was amply covered. Then a "beat" writer of the day, influenced by the Dadaists and described as "Cubist Artist," authored a stream-of-consciousness:

Sturgeon at arms and fur caps. A block. A block sans eggs and beer and fish. Hash and bullocks and coffee. More block. Fish and much fish and too much block. A cigarette or seven. Van Boris Qu. Goodbye.

An bag of oats. Crushed oats and nightmares. Watering troughs with immature coughs. A hate. My such a hate. And deep thoughts. Deep deep thoughts. Daughters and marriage and questions and white haired answers. The tests. The hard tests. And failure. What are brains and

why? An bag of oats. Crushed oats and little birds following. We bid you be well.

(One allusion was to Izzy Block, who represented a New
York Yiddish daily. He weighed 250 lbs. and ate enormous
meals; the other alluded to Daniel Bidwell, a Yale man
who though an accredited ship's correspondent—*Hartford
Courant*—shunned the news crowd. He was virtually the
only newsman who had been on the Western front in
France, was arrested as a spy and held in a military prison
at the Chateau de Boulogne-sur-mer.)

But though the newsmen had swallowed the whole affair
with these grains of salt, it was these very newsmen—those of
them who were left—who, a quarter of a century afterwards,
remembered.

Henry Ford himself had forgotten peace—or so complained
those Peace Ship guests who regularly turned up at Dearborn
to try to work their "contact." These suppliants, who couldn't
accept the fact that the party was over, were given the standard tour of the fabled River Rouge plant. This writer, virtually
having saved his host's life during that early-morning constitutional on the deck of the Oscar, was accorded the type-A tour.
I was guided by Ford himself, and lunched in the executive dining room.

After lunch he took me to see the huge locomotive—the real
thing, not a toy—which he had dismantled and then put together again all by himself. In this session he was buoyant and
bubbling, even garrulous. He was at home and there was no
talk of peace nor peace-talk. We had been in the war almost
four months. It was during this visit that Ford dropped the
faint hint that if I did not already possess one, I should have a
Model T. "Must write to Plantiff (in New York) about it." It
sounded like a promise, and I cherished the idea all the way
home on the long train ride from Detroit.

For the Model T, I was referred, as on the Expedition, to
Gaston Plantiff. (So was Louis Lochner, who never got his

flivver.) Plaintiff was a sadder, wiser, and shrewder man. "We'll *write!*" he assured me earnestly.

Twenty-five years later I got a letter from Ford.

In the "old grad" spirit of a Tank Battalion reunion to eat, drink and reminisce, the newsmen, who never forgot nor forgave, pitched one of these reunions to commemorate the Twenty-Fifth Anniversary (December 4, 1940) of the Ford Peace Ship's departure from Hoboken. A handful of aging survivors showed up at that Overseas Press Club luncheon at the Gladstone Hotel in New York.

Sorely missed was Elmer Davis who was bedded at Sydenham Hospital, New York, but nevertheless summoned his familiar Hoosier humor to greet us by letter:

> Dear Peace de Resistance Fellows:
>
> I regret that an indisposition of a fundamental character prevents me from joining Burnet Hershey, Bert Braley, Arthur Hartzell, Miriam Teichner, Willie Bullitt, and any other snakes in our palm garden who may have assembled to celebrate the melancholy fact that a quarter of a century has passed since we were able to stay up all night for anything but work. . . .
>
> If we still call ourselves the Vacillating Sons of Saint Vitus it may be due more to Parkinson's than to Park & Tilford. However, Time has its compensations, trivial perhaps, but better than nothing. If we can no longer send the bill to Gaston Plantiff, we are at least a little better able to meet it ourselves.
>
> To all the friendly sons and sisters of St. Vitus, I send Greetings, and the more or less encouraging thought that, at any rate, we are never likely to see another World War, since this one with its ramifications will probably last as long as we shall. Nasm!
>
> Elmer Davis

(Davis' last word, "nasm," was an old war cry of the peace party, and is pronounced *nazzum,* the way it looks.)

Newsman Hartzell of the *New York Sun* said the reunion reminded him of the thinning ranks of a G.A.R. encampment —and Louis Lochner, who had just terminated a difficult and memorable assignment as Associated Press correspondent in Hitler's Germany, waxed sentimental and nostalgic.

Although "saluting his fellow voyagers," Henry Ford was absent from this gathering. He sent me a lengthy telegram which, in part, read:

> I am glad that you are observing the 25th anniversary of the sailing of what has been called the Peace Ship. I do not hesitate to say that I learned a great deal on that voyage which has helped me to understand other things that have occurred during these 25 years and it seems to me that with the oceans full of war ships we can afford to remember that there was once a Peace Ship. At least we who sailed in 1915 did not decrease the life or love that was in the world. It is a pleasure after so many years to greet my fellow voyagers on the Oscar 2nd. With all good wishes to everyone of you, I am,
>
> Henry Ford

The next day he followed this up with a personal letter in which he repeated much that was in the telegram. He had really not forgotten the Ship nor had he forgiven the newsmen for the much maligned coverage. He just would not come to the party.

There was no "party" to commemorate the Fiftieth Anniversary in 1966. The truth is there was hardly anyone left to come to it.

14

What's Past is Prologue

The time had arrived for the wrap-up of the Ford peace adventure. It had reached the terminal stage not merely for the strange cargo that had sailed with the Oscar II, but for the hopes and expectations of the chief pilots, Ford and Schwimmer. The war was raging furiously on into its third year and the peace-makers everywhere, mainly in neutral lands, were experiencing something of the frustration suffered by the Ford pilgrims themselves. Many projects for restraining the belligerents together with old and new "cures" for war had gone down the drain, over-advocated, talked out and propagandized to extinction. In America could be heard the distant rumblings of the guns of April.*

Despite the wrack and ruin which bestrewed the Ford Peace Expedition, almost no one understood what had really happened. That a body-blow had been dealt to the salient idea of the neutral arbiter was obvious. The loss of credentials and prestige of the two principal actors had destroyed whatever hope for mediation may still have been around when Henry

* April 6, 1917 the U.S. declared war against Germany.

and Rosika moved on to their separate destinies.

Having been cast in the role of The Great Pacifier and clad with this identity on the front pages of newspapers the world over, where could Ford go from here? What would be his role henceforth? Was he personally concerned with how world opinion looked upon him?

"Even," said U.S. Ambassador to Germany, J. W. Gerard, "if he came to Berlin dressed like a clown in green tights, carrying peace placards and running up and down Wilhelmstrasse shouting 'Peace,' I would say he deserved praise."

So Ford's own countryman damned him with faint praise as a kind of international harlequin. A German, on the other hand, proclaimed, "Ford grew to the proportions of a tragic figure, compared, not without justice, to Gerhard Hauptmann's Emanual Quint." This mythic Teutonic view was expressed by German propagandist Dr. Bernhard Dernberg. It most certainly would have been lost upon Ford.

His own fellow citizens didn't see him as a tragic figure, however, not even as a harlequin or a crusader or a zealot or any of the dozens of labels pinned on him. The one he cared for most and which he admitted was the "accurate epithet" was "Sage of Dearborn." Back home the regional press delighted in digging up such morsels as that Ford was a great admirer of the Michigan National Guard and often went to rifle competitions, presenting a rifle trophy for marksmanship to the militia. "Perhaps," the Detroit editorialist commented, "the first indication of his growing admiration for peace was that he never hit the target."

Dean Marquis, in his study of Henry Ford,* attempts an interpretation. Of his own ambiguous role in the alleged abduction of Ford from Christiania, the Dean remained modestly silent. But he seeks at length to explain what got Ford into the

* (*Shortly after publication, this book became mysteriously unavailable, even at the public library, where it was relegated to categories reserved for D. H. Lawrence and Henry Miller, and other literature of content deemed too heady for anybody not actively working on his doctorate.*)

Peace Ship project, and out of it. He says that Ford was a man "not satisfied with what he has, and with what he is," who was compelled to perform for mankind "a real service," to deliver a *message*. He likens the returning Ford to the singed moth who has danced too close to the flame, but also to the acrobat who simply has so much to fall back on that he is indifferent to a tumble.

"The Dream and the Awakening," one journalist titled her evaluation of Ford's own experience, but how rude actually that awakening we may only construe. To his closest associates, such as Charles Sorensen, he said nothing; publicly he said that he had learned a lot, that he had learned that it was the people themselves who were responsible for perpetuating war. How much bravado and rationalization went into this statement we can only guess.

When Ford landed in New York on January 3, he said, in his interviews with the press, that he had hastened his return because of a touch of the grippe, but that he had told his wife he would be home in about five weeks, and had previously planned to take a steamer which had sailed on the day of his actual return to New York.

He denied warmly that he had deserted the Expedition, lost faith in it, or that there had been any trouble. He said he regretted nothing. "If we can shorten this war by even a single day we will have saved as many men as are employed in our factory turning out 2,000 cars a day. And I believe that the sentiment we have aroused by making the people think will shorten the war. When you get the people thinking, they will think right."

He said the only thing that bothered him at all was that his wife was distressed over the criticisms that had been levelled against him. But he said his son Edsel didn't mind it. "I like it; I hope it won't stop. You know the best fertilizer in the world is weeds."

He said he had gone to Europe personally to show the people that he was willing to give more than his money for the cause of peace. He spoke of his feeling that he was only the custodian of his money, given him by the very men being slaughtered in the trenches.

A new context for this sublime line of thinking was undoubtedly generated for Ford by the talk he heard one evening on board the Oscar, as it was approaching Scandinavian waters. The talk was all about Alfred Nobel and it came from some better informed minds than Henry's who listened, spellbound, to the story of another tycoon who spent a fortune on peace, a man full of conflicts and contradictions, the most amazing of which was his hatred of war because he manufactured explosives. Delegate Thomas Seltzer, a New York book publisher and editor was considering a biography of Nobel at the time and was full of the subject. What excited and fascinated Ford were certain transparencies with his own achievements and aims; lowly beginnings, rise to wealth and power through hard work and native acumen, a contempt for the world of Big Business and finance and ("By jiminy crickets, we're like birds of a feather") Nobel's pledge of his fortune for peace!

It was an enthralling kaffee-klatch, with a half-dozen of the ship's intellectuals sounding off with some elementary psychoanalytical notions—even pre-Freudian—about Nobel's *"guilt complex";* the inventor of dynamite who wanted to atone for his impiety by conferring a peace prize. Since Henry had served neither Mars nor Mammon, this analysis was evidently over his head. All he wanted to know was the amount of dollars the prize winner collected. According to Seltzer, he was not impressed by the $35,000 figure. Still, some of the sycophants in his midst thought they would butter him up by hinting there was a good chance he himself might be a candidate for the Peace Prize, and in such illustrious company as those earlier American recipients, Theodore Roosevelt and Elihu Root. It was Seltzer's recollection that he heard something which sounded like a characteristic Ford reaction: *"Me* get this peace prize? Heck, I'll *give* one of my own."

Prize or no prize, he said he'd go back to Europe, if necessary. He said, if it would help matters, he'd charter another ship.

"Did you come back to try to get official backing?" one reporter asked him.

"No," said Ford, "I think the officials are the weakest of the lot. They're afraid of their jobs, and that's what I told them in Norway."

"Do you include the Washington Administration in your condemnation?"

"Fix it any way you like," said Ford. "You will anyway."

Then he spoke of his belief that the people themselves were blameworthy, for throwing their electoral support to the wrong leaders. Henry Ford had become political. He would come up with a denunciation of preparedness. "I am against preparedness, because preparedness means war."

Meanwhile, in Europe, Lochner, eager for anything to get the Expedition back on the front page, was getting conflicting reports about whether Ford was coming back and whether William Jennings Bryan was to become a delegate. It is Lochner's conviction to this day that Ford was ready to return, at least for the opening of the conference, but was dissuaded by his associates, who also gave Bryan such a brush-off that the latter did not feel he could with dignity join the conference. Lochner, of course, felt that prospects for the concrete work of the Expedition were thus being cut down by inches.

But at the time of Mme. Schwimmer's resignation, at the opening of the conference in Stockholm, early in March 1916, Ford's watchdog secretary Liebold cabled, "Assure delegates of Mr. Ford's interest and cooperation and extend his compliments." Ford was later to say that Mme. Schwimmer had more brains than all the rest on the Peace Ship, and he defended her long afterwards when she sued a columnist for saying that

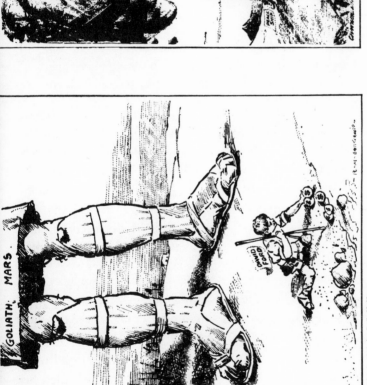

"NOW, YOU STOP!"

—Chamberlain in the New York *Evening Sun*.

Copyrighted. 1915. by S. S. McClure.

"WELL, DAVID DID IT."

—Brinkerhoff in the New York *Evening Mail*.

A NOBLE, IF NOT A NOBEL, PURPOSE.

Ford's anti-Semitism originated in her misappropriation of Peace Ship funds.

While rapport between the conference in Europe and himself declined, Ford was nonetheless active for peace at home. On February 23 he ran his first full-page anti-preparedness advertisement. In this he pointed out, among other trenchant data, that scientist Hudson Maxim's alarmist book *Defenseless America* was published just before Maxim put the stock of his munition company on the market.

In June President Wilson called out the National Guard (which of course included Michigan men) over the Mexican border raids instigated by Pancho Villa. Eventually, Villa was chased home by General Pershing and Ford was moved to give out a statement:

> We should be sorry to see any of our men resign or enlist in the National Guard, but both recruits and State militiamen will be treated alike—as though they quit the plant to engage in other lines of business.

This brought down the wrath of many Americans upon his head. But in the same month, Gaston Plantiff was dispatched to the Stockholm conference, to "meddle," as Lochner put it. The conference was to be transferred to The Hague, and the budget cut to the bone. It did seem that the whole project was to be killed by degrees, and that Ford, as he himself had said, really felt he was needed most at home to fight against armament. Lochner, a pacifist in all details of life, was especially bitter that the German border guards took apart his little daughter's baby-doll in their search of the luggage.

In September, Lochner was summoned home, on two hours' notice, and in New York he was told by Ford simply to go see the Kaiser. He was to "get the Kaiser to disarm." "Tell him I'll back him to the limit," Ford told Lochner.

This was more Ford's style. A world war was something to be settled "between me and Kaiser Bill." The conference had

A PEACE ANGEL — IS NOT ALWAYS — A BROADWAY ANGEL

At Least He Doesn't Show Any Flutterings That Way, as Indicated by His Refusal to Buy Pretty Gowns for Women Pilgrims.

gotten too academic, abstract, and complicated for him. In a recapitulation, Lochner, or any of the conference delegates, might have said, as in the Carroll poem:

> I said it in Hebrew—I said it in Dutch—
> I said it in German and Greek:
> But I wholly forgot (and it vexes me much)
> That English is all that you speak.

Ford had remarked that the peace committee program was "news to me." His comments on the whole venture grew increasingly cool. He said the ship had been Jane Addams' idea, and of William Jennings Bryan he said, "I hardly know the man." Sara Moore's question, "Is Henry Ford getting measured for a dunce cap or a halo?" was answered by one cartoonist showing the woman delegates, for whose conference-opening gowns he had declined to pay, appealing to Ford who was winging rapidly off into the clouds with his harp, singing 'Good night, ladies."

But when it came to direct confrontations, whether with the Kaiser or the President of the United States, Louis Lochner was no slouch either, and with zeal unabated and "Ford's blessing," was to tackle both dignitaries in rapid succession. The conference was to be transformed into an "International Commission." Almost simultaneously a Berlin peace note and a Wilson peace note were issued. "Peace" talk pervaded the air for a brief moment and everybody had his own peace-fish to fry. The President was full of his League of Nations plan. The reason, of course, that everybody was suddenly so hot for peace was that the war was getting hotter and hotter.

As late as January 7, Henry Ford sent a telegram to a preparedness meeting at the Republican Club of New York saying in part, "An army or navy is a tool for the protection of misguided, inefficient, destructive Wall Street."

But on February 3, the United States broke off diplomatic relations with Germany. Ford had painted himself into a corner. He did not have, and never had had, the firm philosophical basis for his pacifism from which Lochner and the others drew their inexhaustible detachment. Lochner genuinely was "dazed" to find himself fired without notice, and not by Ford personally, but by the very man circumvention of whom had made the Peace Expedition possible—Liebold.

The business-is-business attitude of Ford's top secretary made the young peace-secretary's blood run cold. It simply made sense, Liebold explained, matter-of-factly, for Ford to offer the Government his plant for munitions manufacture, rather than wait for it to be commandeered.

"Henry Ford deserted his ship," Lochner commented sadly. "He was tried in the balance and found wanting."

Ford's own position was incomprehensible to the absolute pacifist, Lochner stated.

"When our country entered the war, it became the duty of every citizen to do his utmost toward seeing through to the end that which we had undertaken. I believe that it is the duty of the man who opposes war to oppose going to war up until the time of its actual declaration. My opposition to war is not based upon pacifist or non-resistant principles."

But Ford never ceased to reiterate his opposition to war, although he conceded that in the present state of civilization, fighting might be required to get the participants ready to negotiate.

Ford's war-effort was no more successful than his peace-effort. Typically, he developed "one-man" tanks and submarines; the model T had gone to war, to be rejected by both the Army and the Navy. Ford tried to apply his single great idea to everything, including war and peace. The Navy took his particular pride—his Eagle-boat, a kind of small submarine-chaser, calculated to make the most seasoned salt seasick—possibly to keep Ford quiet, and lived to regret it. In fact, from a less ingenuous manufacturer, Ford's war-effort might have looked more like sabotage.

With another of his flamboyant public gestures, Ford announced that he would sell to the Government at cost. At this the few minority stockholders set up a hue and cry—this was carrying patriotism too far. So Ford offered the Government instead every cent from his own 58.5%. This never came to pass, but in some quarters it redounded to Ford's reputation for public-spiritedness. From pacifists on both sides of the Atlantic there was an outcry of "Shame, shame, Henry Ford!"

But he always stuck to his guns—to use a Fordian mixed metaphor—on his Peace Ship or off it. Later, after the war, he insisted that it had been his belief, on the basis of information given him at the time of the Expedition, that a favorable climate for such a demonstration for peace existed. "I do not now

The New York Daily Mirror,
25 years later, March 10, 1940.

SYMBOL OF THE HOPE FOR PEACE that swept the
25 years ago was this poster, which hung on the side of the
Ford "Peace Ship." Ford's friends tried to discourage th
but Ford backed Mme. Schwimmer and her Peace Mission
abandoned the idea a week after the ship landed in Norwa
mission went on bravely but hopelessly in the face of i
feuding and constant sneering by the newspapers, finally e
in Holland in 1916. A generation later, Walter Millis,
"Road to War," wrote: "...The 'Peace Ship'...one of th
really generous and rational impulses of those insane yea
been snuffed out with a cruelty and a levity which were app
Shortly before the "Peace Ship" sailed, President Wilson
from Mme. Schwimmer the idea for a Neutral Mediation C
ence, and gave it his unofficial blessing. While the Oscar
still on the sea, Wilson delivered his first Preparedness m
to Congress, started the U. S. on the Road to War.

THE WOMEN in the International Congress which Mme. Schwimmer and Jane Addams brought together to force peace on war-mad Europe in 1914, represented belligerent as well as neutral nations. Here (left to right) are Emily G. Balch of the U. S., Mme. Cor Ramondt from Holland, Mme. Schwimmer of Hungary, and Crystal Macmillan of England. They are in front of the Royal Palace at Oslo, Norway, where King Haakon had told them a few minutes before that he would work for peace by trying to line up neutral nations. "But," he added a little discouragingly, "I have only one vote."

SCAR'

RAZZBERRY," bit-idicule from hard-cynics, has always Peace Drives once a egan. And the ranks Pacifists have always plit by bickering feuds—rgets for the Razzberry. was the story of the pectacular Peace Drive of t war, conceived by the g Roskia Schwimmer, rian feminist and news-oman. Selling point for Push for Peace was her s warning to Wilson: ou do not help us end the before the militarists end J, too, will be in..." king with America's Jane s, Mme. Schwimmer in rded 2,000 militant women s to the Hague, and de-an immediate "Neutral ence for Continuous ion." Carried personally belligerents by Miss Ad-to the neutrals by Mme. amer, the demand drew replies from four Allied, oral assurances from ermanic Powers. Deeply sed, Henry Ford poured $500,000 into the resulting Push, helped finance the Peace Ship—Oscar II. Oscar, bulging beneath ace pilgrims, sailed from ork to Norway on Dec. 4, No submarines, no mine l the Oscar—a jeering the same old razzberry d the Oscar's mission in ne of "Realism."

TODAY, Mme. Schwimmer lives quietly in N. Y., works for a World Constitutional Convention to end the present war. She calls the Welles peace trip "silly . . . Stop war first, then decide what each nation needs. Don't as`  ghters what they want w` hey fight. They always it the impossible."

HENRY FORD'S MONEY launched the famous but futile Oscar II in 1915. Aboard the boat were the peace pilgrims, college students and co-eds, several ministers, and stowaway Irving Caesar, now fame song writer. Today Ford refus to answer an appeal from me. Scwhimmer for a new world peace move.

know whether the information as conveyed to me was true or false. I do not care. But I think everyone will agree that if it had been possible to end the war in 1916, the world would be better off than it is today . . . I had hoped, finally, when the United States entered the war, that it might be a war to end wars, but now I know that wars do not end wars any more than an extraordinarily large conflagration does away with the fire hazard."

As Lochner observed, "One cannot escape the conclusion that Ford himself never fully grasped the idea that he championed, and that his peace campaign (like his anti-Semitic propaganda, his political aspirations, and his adventures in currency reform later) was merely the passing whim of a man who, elated by his successes as an inventor and manufacturer, went far beyond his depth when dabbling in statesmanship." This conclusion was strengthened by Henry Ford's book, *My Life and Work*. Less than 14 lines in that volume of 200 pages are devoted to a brief and superficial mention of the Peace Ship. Not a word is said about the earnest, promising work which was carried on by the unofficial Neutral Conference for Continuous Mediation and the Ford International Commission, which Ford left behind and even paid for in part.

H. G. Wells, who had been duly appreciative of the Ford Expedition, and particularly of Rosika Schwimmer's role in it, wrote in his book, *The Shape of Things to Come*, ". . . A certain Madame Rosika Schwimmer, a Hungarian lady, gleams forth and vanishes again from history as the organizing spirit of this selection." (The Ford Peace Expedition)

But Rosika was not the kind of character who "vanishes" from history or anything else. For better and for worse, she remained on the scene, very much in the public domain, although she was convinced that her efforts to save the Ford Neutral Conference were futile. For almost two years she sat out the remaining bloody chapters of the war and the American participation in it. As a citizen of a belligerent nation, she chose to sit under a neutral umbrella. Stockholm and The Hague still felt her crusading presence but with diminished fervor. A deep melancholia, a symptom of her mounting anguish over the incredible casualties, had set in and slowed her up.

After Hungary's defeat, in October 1918, Rosika knew it was time for her to go home, back to Budapest where she was welcomed joyfully and not put to "vanishment." The pacifist-liberal Count Michael Karolyi appointed her a member of the Hungarian National Council, and only a month later his Cabinet designated her as Minister to Switzerland, the first woman ambassador in history. When the Karolyi government fell to the Communists, she was asked to remain in her post, but refused. She was then denied her civil rights and refused permission to leave her country.

It was at this time that prophet Wells was correct: Rosika was in danger of her life, in danger of vanishing forever, if she did not escape. In February 1920, with the help of English and American Quakers, Swedish relief missionaries, a member of the British parliament, and other friends, she was smuggled out of red Hungary on a Danube boat to Vienna.

Rosika, back in the United States in 1921, was not the healthy, confident, invincible woman of the Peace Ship days. Her unsparing efforts to save the work of the Ford Conference and, now her political exile, was too much for her. She was seriously ill with a complicated case of diabetes. Added to this was an unprecedented barrage of vicious misrepresentation which greeted her arrival in America. It was the work of alleged "fringe" organizations which were pledged to keep the U.S. militarized to the limit. To them the once-powerful Rosika was an enemy, and everything had to be done, no matter how unconscionable, to discredit her.

These organizations circulated that Mme. Schwimmer was a "German spy," a "Bolshevik agent," a "swindler," an "adventuress." No lie was too wild or too filthy to be spread, and they succeeded in damaging her reputation so that she was unable to earn her living in her profession of journalism and lecturing.

At this point Rosika Schwimmer, "Citizen of the World," as she was described, came back into the headlines as the heroine of a genuine *cause celebre,* an American affair which made her role on the Peace Ship appear unimportant by comparison. Her original application for U.S. citizenship was turned down by the District Court in Chicago when she refused to "take up arms in defense of the country" (although America's women have never been called on to use arms on the battlefronts). The homeless, ailing Rosika was paying a dear price for her "notorious" role in the Ford Expedition. On a wave of newspaper editorials, cartoons, protest meetings and petitions, the case was carried to a higher court.

Irate citizens and organizations anxious to preserve the American tradition of freedom of conscience, appealed in her behalf to the higher court, and then came a brief spell of success. The U.S. Court of Appeals ordered Rosika's citizenship granted. But the Labor Department, in whose jurisdiction naturalization matters belong, had her case reversed in the U.S. Supreme Court, in a 6–3 decision, on May 27, 1929.

Justice Oliver Wendell Holmes, writing the dissenting opinion which became a classic, had as his concurring allies Justices Brandeis and Sanford: "The applicant," wrote Holmes, "seems to be a woman of superior character and intelligence, obviously more than ordinarily desirable as a citizen of the United States." Although she remained stateless, those words were a tonic to Rosika.

More heartwarming encouragement came from the people and the press. In the *New York Journal American* of June 4 1929, William Randolph Hearst penned an indignant, scathing editorial indicting the six "reactionary judges" who had delivered this "outrageously un-American decision to bar Mrs. Schwimmer . . ."

But organizations like the American Legion saluted the Supreme Court Decision. "Henry Ford mended his ways and became a war patriot. Why can't his old pal?" they asked in denunciation of "pal" Schwimmer.

Rosika, a lady who had a right to change her mind, never did. She remained ardently loyal to her pacifist ideals which included the goal of world disarmament. She remained stateless, but was befriended by many Americans with whom she lived and who dispensed her literature advocating a world federation of nations.

Conspicuously absent from her ring of friends was Henry Ford, a silent ally of the past on whose ship she had sailed with never a qualm about what horizon Fate had in store. Their Messianic partnership had dissolved into a mess.

A half century had literally flown by—a half century of wars, revolutions and man-made disasters which had taken its toll of whole countries, rulers, statesmen, diplomats and entire populations. With the passing of these years many ideas had changed, new problems had appeared, but the problem of making peace, or stopping wars remained where it was when Ford and his pilgrims sailed for Europe.

The Expedition ended the way it began—a tale of a foolish pilgrimage, a sublimely screwy paragraph in American history. Only the newspaper reporters who accompanied Ford on this lush junket emerged unscarred. They were the only true realists, although their cynicism helped to wreck the "Peace Chase" with a cruelty and levity which was unique in American newspaper reporting. And possibly a measure of the world's scorn for Ford's Peace Ship may be attributed in part to the fact that he had the means to buy a larger share than anyone else in the world-wide failure—the failure then and since "to get the boys out of the trenches."

THE TAB (*An approximate account*)

Biltmore headquarters (organization costs)	$ 35,000
Passages on Oscar II	49,000
Tips on Oscar	5,000
Wireless messages from Oscar	10,000
Hotel bills in Christiania, including banquet	35,000
Tips in Christiania	4,000
Donations in Christiania ($10,000 to Norwegian Students association & $5,000 to poor)	15,000
Xmas gifts, clothes, charged to Ford	7,500
Taxis in Christiania (no Fords available)	2,000
Railroad fares from Christiania to Stockholm	2,000
Meals on train	1,000
Tips on train	100
Hotel bills in Stockholm, including banquet	50,000
Tips in Stockholm	5,000
Gifts in Stockholm to various organizations for charity and "peace promotion"	28,000
Taxis in Stockholm	2,000
Railroad fares Stockholm to Copenhagen	2,500
Meals on train	1,500
Tips on train	200
Hotel bills in Copenhagen, including banquet	40,000
Tips in Copenhagen	4,000
Donations in Copenhagen	15,000
Taxis in Copenhagen	2,000
Railroad fares through Germany from Copenhagen and The Hague	2,400
Meals on train	1,500
Tips on train	200
Hotel bills in The Hague	35,000
Tips in The Hague	4,000
Railroad fares (delegate travel to and fro) Norway, Sweden and Holland	3,000
Cables from land points	20,000
Printing, posters, etc.	25,000
"Loans" to delegates (pocket money)	20,000
Medical bills and undertaker	3,600
Insurance policies	4,800
Damage indemnities	3,000
Salaries paid in Europe	15,000
Equipment—typewriters, duplicating machinery, etc.	9,500
Stationery	6,000
Incidentals	8,000
Passage home	40,000
Tips on steamer home	4,000
	$520,800 °

° Represents a 100 cent gold dollar.

A Selective Bibliography

CROWTHER, SAMUEL and FORD, HENRY. *My Life and Work*. New York: Doubleday Co., 1923

Dearborn Independent, 1929

LOCHNER, LOUIS. *America's Don Quixote*. London: Kegan-Paul, 1923

NEVINS, ALLAN and HILL, F. E. *Ford: Expansion & Challenge*. New York: Charles Scribner's Sons, 1957

RANDALL, MERCEDES M. *Improper Bostonian*. New York: Twayne Publishers, 1964

RUDIMEN, MARGARETE. "*Memories of My Brother*," (History of Michigan Vol. 37-Sept. 1953)

SORENSEN, CHARLES. *My Forty Years With Ford*. New York: W. W. Norton, 1956

STEFFENS, LINCOLN. *Autobiography*. New York: Harcourt, Brace, 1936

TUCHMAN, BARBARA, *The Guns of August,* New York: Macmillan Co., 1962

Index

212

Swain, Maxwell, *147*
Sweden, *see Stockholm*

Taft, William Howard, 27
Tagbladet, 133
Talleyrand, Charles Maurice de, 30
Tannenbaum, Frank, 51
Tarbell, Ida, 26
Teichner, Miriam, 188
Tirpitz, Alfred von, 108–109
Tisza, Count Stephen, 67
Tisza Tales, 84, 98
Tolstoi, Leo, 54
Toscanini, Arturo, 3
Trevelyan, George, 49

U-boats, 11, 94, 98, 108–110
United Irish Societies, 46
United Nations, 63
United Press, 147
United States Communist party, 51
Unity, 71

Vacillating Sons of St. Vitus, *see Ancient & Honorable Order of the Vacillating Sons of St. Vitus*
Vassar College, 13
Villa, Pancho, 196
Villard, Oswald Garrison, 17, 21, 50
Viviani, René, 67

Wales, Julia Grace, 64–66
Wanamaker, John, 22, 26, 27
War Babies' Cradle, 46
War Memoirs, 62
War and Peace, 54
Warnemuende, 163–164
Warren, Mrs. Whitney, 12
Webster, Jean, 3
Wellesley, 23, 66, 104
Wells, H. G., 66, 202, 203
Wilson, Carolyn, *147*
Wilson, Margaret, 26
Wilson, Woodrow, meeting with Lochner, 14; and Ford, 17–21, 36, 154; policy, 31–32, 47–48, 88–89, 94, 98, 100–102, 109, 196; and Schwimmer, 63, 68–69
Wisconsin, University of, 64
Wise, Stephen S., 26, 174
Wister, Owen, 49, 58, 60–61
"With Master Minds," 98
Women's Peace Party, 63
Women's International League for Peace and Freedom, 50, 118
Women's International Peace Conference, 118, 175
Woolsey, Theodore Salisbury, 174

Yasnaya Polyana, 54

Zero, Mr., *see Urban Ledoux*